THE MIRACLE SHED

The Miracle Shed

PHILIP MACCANN

◊

faber and faber

LONDON · BOSTON

First published in 1995
by Faber and Faber Limited
3 Queen Square London wc1n 3au

Phototype set by Datix International, Bungay, Suffolk
Printed and bound in Great Britain by
Mackays of Chatham plc, Chatham, Kent

A CIP record for this book is
available from the British Library

ISBN 0–571–17322–5

Tender first appeared in *New Writing 1* (Minerva, 1992).
Harvestman first appeared in *New Writing 3* (Minerva, 1994).
Grey Area first appeared in *First Fictions:
Introduction 11* (Faber and Faber, 1992).
Dark Hour first appeared in *The New Yorker*.
A version of *Love Marks* first appeared in *Winter's Tales,
New Series 10* (Constable, 1994).

2 4 6 8 10 9 7 5 3 1

CONTENTS

The author wishes to acknowledge the
kind assistance of the Arts Council
of Northern Ireland.

. . . a great variety of morbid symptoms appears.
Gramsci

I

TENDER

————————

I JUST RECENTLY have cut in through Hardwicke Street. A person can't forget this inner city. I was on my way to my pal's place and I cut in. Stay with me. A person in the first place says what comes to them, those things that make up their lifestyle, like walking down Hardwicke Street one evening for a thing to do. Don't get me wrong. I wasn't looking for something to love. That's not me.

This slum was wearing the blue-black punched out by the lamps, but with a dignity that I can believe is the start of poems. Pearliness. I was coming up to some tiny kids. This is a broad concrete street, Catholic, there are toys on the ground. Darkish, brightish, not showy, but sort of classy mizzle was lapping against these Georgian grim hard houses like sick water. I was being stared at. One of those fucking babies shouted out towards me. My skin crept tighter over my bones. For one or another reason I wanted to use the word 'pearliness', even if it is a lie, and even if there is nothing to make this place worth more than a bit of its own dogshit. This is the poorest place you've ever seen. This is a poor city I walk around in. Still, there is something down here that gets me thinking of a feeling like pearliness. I walked brisk past these kids. But one of them started to stroll along beside me. A baby. My chest had become a toy drum. My legs were lumpish and truculent, they wanted to turn around and waddle back.

'Hey, mister!' the kid said. I looked down. He was far down. His face was pale. I am surprised that such faces don't get bruised on the dusk. 'What're you lookin' for?' There was glass under my feet, crushing deliciously. I wanted to be out of this electricity at once, its dark sparkle, caustic and blue, and the smell of wild light, distracted, fresh and smoky. I wanted to be elsewhere. Perhaps I belong in this air. I belong in that bunched-up bit of messy cloud, it's free. Cloud, I think, you and I have something in common. 'Are you lookin' for somethin'?' that kid asked. He was poor, his brown belly was showing. I like that cloud. We've taken to each other so fast. I like it because it crosses my mind to tell me I understand nothing. Where is this infant's mother? Some old tart, nowhere, I can't imagine who she is, she's tumbling by with the stars, anyway. But I know nothing, right? I don't care what I want, do I. I don't know what I'm looking for, do I. And everything I feel and everything that eats into me, they mean spit, don't they. Added up together and with the compound interest of my screams, they all amount to as much as a wisp. That kid stopped his walking beside me so I breathed a fat relief. Now you see it doesn't have any more importance than the wisp I referred to, let me continue to tell you what I got from this here Hardwicke Street.

Make sure you can picture the air. It had flung on a moody shirt. It had struck a pose that it knew well was both a pose and seductive, and guaranteed to buzz through you if you were new to this place or didn't know a thing or two about air. Air can be treacherous. But take it easy, it has a lot of business to see to, a lot on its mind, a lot of houses to prop up and such like. Now there were young men doing their bit to hold a wall in place up ahead. Mere boys. But understand: that wall needed them. I was getting near when a stone hit my back. Those babies were still messing about with my discarded footsteps. They began shouting out. 'You fuckin' rapist.' That's what they shouted out. I got

4

tense. Tense. We were all together inside a drizzle. And clinging to the drizzle was opalescence. I recognized it. 'Opalescence!' I wanted to yell, to test it very loud. Interesting that so delicate a word should refer here to no more than needles and pins which have learned to fly. 'What's he want?' a mouth somewhere behind me said. I kept walking towards the boys. I learned then I have hackles. The shortest boy could bolt right through you if you itched in the wrong direction. I had to concentrate. For me, broken bottle glass and corner walls and the accent of the kids had already begun to tap infinity. It only takes the wink of that sharp corner, you could tell yourself, less, the mere sight of a broken flagstone, that puddle of oily sky, for you to get tangled up for ever in these images. Your foot will get caught up inside one. The darkening appeal of all this wants to trick us, it's got me by the hand now and is telling me now that I belong here in this gentle hardness. Better be careful if you're down here. Act right.

'Right?'

'Right.'

Together these boys had all the different faces necessary to protect a wall. I won't deny that around these slum streets you can see the diverse novelty of the animal and how dirty it is. There are too many details down here to carry away on your shoulders. I still had those infant words, 'What's he want?' sticking to me like tape. Now I looked back at the boys. Oddly, I caught sight of two souvenirs: eyes, crude things, like trinkets of eyes. Two unmistakables, impudent and patient, got themselves half hooked on my glimpse. They wanted to be in my collection of reality. The night was a wall and these were two stones in it. But they were malevolent pieces, with eyelashes of light. I tramped on with my collection dead slow. Follow this: I'm weak anyway with feeling what a zonked-out stone we're living on. Now I was obliging all those broken bottles and an invalid flagstone which had attached themselves to me for the ride, as

5

well as two children's severed voices, as well as the cloud wetly
pestering my back. So now I've got these additional two curios
and the whole weight is all just enough to make my neck lapse.

I looked round again. This blond idiot was snuggling his back
up against the kind wall.

'Right?'

'Yeah.'

'What's he lookin' at?'

'Cool it, kid.' Here I caught another flash of that tarty
deliberate look. I walked on.

I was coming to the square. The babies had melted probably
now or become brick. All around sight was getting soupy and
eye-level ink leaves were twitching. This body of mine was
angry now. I climbed my angry way up the city along the
square, through sparkling chimney smoke, under the dusty spread
of trees, vandalized trunks. I strolled through where it all tumbles
down in sliced houses, wallpaper, fireplaces overhanging you. It's
not a good town, this big town. I don't recommend it. If things
were my way you would never get these mere teenagers standing
about arsechatting to the breeze anyway. I was turning over the
pieces I'd taken away and trying to comprehend them. That kid
had got something seriously wrong. This is a sick place. It's
imploring you to burn it. In the general run of most things that
look had only one meaning. Somebody ought to rub us out. If I
could get my hands on a fat, city-sized, colossal-sized rubbing-out
instrument I'd just nicely rub out the whole bad picture. I don't
belong here. It's only out to trick you, the charm of this sketchy
city, it's a real photogenic grainy type of limbo, built brick for
brick out of dark light. I'd like to start again on a new picture. I
can redesign a better place. Don't doubt it. I'd use buckets of
colour. Pure blood purple. Tear white. I'd spring-clean the secrets
out of those lampblack trees in Denmark Street and Hardwicke
Street too. Now I was coming near where I aimed to be, a house

on Dominick Street. I tell you, this was a poor situation. My pal, I thought, better have some money. He better have some money, I thought. So we can get ourselves pissed, I hoped. I felt like a wild row could start. By me, namely. Maybe I had a little short circuit. I came to the house on Dominick Street.

I threw open the door. I walked straight up the stairs to where my pal has his little home. 'Hi,' I said. 'Look who it is, my fucking self,' I said. I was expecting him to trumpet, 'No problem,' as I entered and fly a flag made of cash. This is what he would say and how he would accompany his speech. But he didn't say anything, just hugged his knees up on the bed and resembled a bald, neckless piece of pond life.

I looked to the window at an oblong of pure lead air. 'Did you score?' I said. This pal was leaning back against the wall in his black plastic jacket looking like some activity was going on behind his eyes on the level of a huff.

'No,' he said. 'There's been some bullshit.'

Well that's a way of my understanding we've sweet nothing to do with ourselves.

'What'll we do?' I said.

'Kill time,' he said.

'How?'

One thing we've been known to do when life gets this degree of tedious is this: we connect up to the gas. Gas doesn't cost any inconvenience and nothing in hard currency beyond the cost of life. But gas can make you sleep on whiskery laughs, soft thumps, threadlike things. He was into the plan. He went over to his makeshift boxroom toilet and rolled out a pig-headed canister from its sleep. He had a tube in his hand and he rammed it on to the snout. In that state of mind right then I would either breathe gas or else not know what to do with my particular self. I got down on my knees. 'I'll go first,' I said. I stuffed the end of that tube between my teeth and released the knob on the canister top.

I fear the smell, I should admit. The smell is the boss, you obey him, he doesn't mess about. I would say gas is a bossy drink of petrol, where colours hide, magenta and green, coin white, budgerigar, golden fist, as far as smell is concerned. But take my word for it, the taste is a fast boot to the head straight away. When you sniff gas you're looking up the definition of a complicated word: brain. You find out whereabouts in life that idea hides itself and what it should do that it isn't doing right then. I fumbled with one big palm-sized toe to turn off, then floated back in a blind blue. This is where I belong, I think: in gas, outside of everything, in nowhere.

When I came round I recollected one of my beliefs. I think gas is made for us. Gas slots into the spaces in your brain. Brain and gas. They both have the same deep structure from the point of view of the chemistry of peace. I believe a better person is in that gas and when you come round you're not yourself so much as maybe half or lots of fractions of a self that add up to a half. Don't be too mathematical about it. This issue here is success. Coming round to this pokey room in Dominick Street in that gas afterglow is like you've left half yourself behind in the black, your happier half.

I asked my pal, 'Did you get a hit?' He answered, 'All right. Did you?' I told him, 'I fell asleep.' We lay about. The dimness was more ultramarine now, real gloom now with cartoons fleeting in it, purples swelling. The pal was just a shadow against the wall above his bed. I let my underground gaspipe mind put my own choice of eyes and mouth on him and plenty of sequins. Already that image of eyes from earlier was returning, in soft focus, a kind of pillow of sleep over it, seemingly, thankfully not trying to worry my numb limbs. I lay relaxed. Then, soon, I spoke. My voice was big in the room, loud, the corners woke up with sore ears.

'What'll we do now?' I didn't expect a reply. I didn't mean it. Being frank about it, I mean one word just as little as another. But just as passionately, too. So, I repeated it. 'What'll we do now?' The shadow of my pal moved, got up and slugged some milk from a carton, looking out of the window.

'Do something,' he said.

'What?'

'Huh.'

When he sat down again he was not so much his own shadow any longer. He shook his fat slow head, but I still was messing about with it and the darkness, putting on him extraterrestrial features, fish lips, swollen moony cranium. He now was one of those superior beings who ought to teach us one or two things when they drop by.

'Drop into Maureen,' he said. He hoisted himself tall. He was jealous of my earlier image of that rich flag. 'C'mon.'

It wasn't easy standing up. The way I got into my coat was like he was forcing me to shake its hand. 'I can pay her back tomorrow when I get some stuff,' he said. 'Come on, she'll give us a suck. You know Maureen.' He gave the door of his cardboard room a sharp flap behind him to close it and we headed on out the door and down Dominick Street for a suck. I was mildly high still. I had a headache. The air reminded my head of its swollen importance. Don't underestimate the regrets of ingesting fuel of an evening. My innards were quivering under my raincoat. We climbed up towards 63B where Maureen is on that stinking old street that leads out of the city, a sewer of all-night shops and rubbish piles, bins. We were walking back up the way I had come down, past the half-houses, the doors ajar overhead, billboard pictures of our Earth or babies, all that stuff. The important point now is light. The light in this town is quite particular to this town, I suspect. There's a certain way it's dark here. In fact, I know the precise word which describes the property of this town's light. The light in this town is oleaginous.

'Come on,' said my pal. I was slacking. A crisp packet had begun to heel along beside me. Amazingly. It was loyal. When it panted on ahead of me it waited for me to catch up, then we carried on at the same pace more or less. Me and this crisp packet. But I was lagging behind the pal. We were just passing the turn for Denmark Street. I got a pang. The misted far end of the street ebbed inside me like a violet ocean. My head was sore, it was a headstone made of granite and cracked through the middle. I stopped. He stopped and looked round at me. The crisp packet went off for its own life.

'I've something to do,' I said. 'I'll come along to Maureen's in five minutes.'

'What?'

'I'll see you there,' I said.

'What?'

'Fuck off,' I said.

He walked away. I cut up the side street on my own into the inner city again.

I can re-emphasize a few points. Concerning this inner city, the word oleaginous is key. As you proceed through this town the buildings slide past in oil. It's a deep-sea town, submerged. You don't live in this shit place. You pass. You have a pass style, but without the style. You slip along in a kind of semi-swim posture with redundant eyes because light doesn't filter down, slip along dim-sightedly, weightily. Oleaginously. We don't belong to our eyes, we don't need them. There was some evil, real oily mist on the street. I came to a corner and turned it. Here was the street along the square. This wasn't far from that wall at the end of Hardwicke Street. A scream sounded far away. I could only just distinguish from the conspiratorial mist camouflaged as street, a huddle of kids along the railing under the million dry twigs and pungent leaves poking out. Tracksuits, dulled red and dulled green, and little pallid faces watching me pass. I saw tiny little soft movements. This is a kingdom of dirty necks. I was coming up to that wall now. I looked round at the kids to see if they were watching me now. But they were too well cloaked. Any second the wall would come up now. I was expecting a stone in my back. The wall was coming marginally too fast forward. Inside me things hugged together, kidney-coloured stones, lung-shaped edges, whatever was down there in my submarine unknown inside bits. I was expecting to be pounced on. My legs were weak. I was dissolving. I reached the corner where those young yobs had their wall, the corner round which that little guy's image was leaning like a kink in the brick. My chest had already become hypnotized by the ritual of a tom-tom. As I walked round I kept my head low. When I had passed it I glanced back casually. Then I was surprised. I thought I might see that picture from earlier, that artful statuesque ease. I wanted to check something against my knowledge of life. I wanted to check I had seen those eyes right. But there was no one there. I walked on. I walked up towards Hardwicke Street, heading towards Maureen's place.

My body was getting heavy. A sidelong block of flats peeped between the Georgian houses. I was hard to carry. There was an alley with smoke in it that led to those scarred flats. My body was in a sulk. As I walked towards the big street I glanced up that alley that led to the flats. Then, all at once, this body of mine turned up that alley. It had a feeling about those flats. It wanted to see those eyes again, I believe.

I walked slowly. Carefully. There was no sound. This body wasn't brave, it was tense to shuddering point. It was ready to sprint back at the softest signal. The smell of smoke pulled a gentle commotion right up to the outside edge of me, it was swirling like filthy milk through me, a blond grime. The court-yard of these flats was quiet and wide. But it wasn't easy to see things. Maybe I would love to belong here, I think. But I can't see that. I can't get my head round that improbability. There were trots from an invisible dog. It emerged. Behind the blocks a taller tower stood. I know this, not because it could be seen, but because of a few dim lights hooked up on the fog. Suddenly I heard a scraping sound. My body jumped an inch out of me. There was a child on a skateboard. He skated up to me. He was a small kid.

I looked around to see if anyone could hear my pulse. I know nothing about the young. I can't imagine their lives. I tried to as I looked at this kid. He had a loud track suit, beginnings of a downy moustache on a baby-face. I couldn't. I couldn't push my imagination out far enough to include a detail like, for example, this child eating, or that boy's leg from earlier walking away from the wall. My dreams only go so far. My body was rigid. Let me put it this way. A flaxen image had got caught in the machinery of my day-to-day thinking. It had damaged some of my equipment. I need to understand that image. I need to be rid of it. I need to pacify it. This is what happened next.

The kid spoke through a flute of a voice. 'Are you lookin' for rent?' I just walked, ignoring him. He was short even on his skateboard. 'What d'you want?' I was juddering. I stopped. His blackberry hair was a wild clump. While he looked up at me he was persisting at a cut on his hand. Its paleness glowed. It was time for me to split from here. If I was patient I would forget in time the idea of complicated eyes. I'd see how crude they are in the reality outside of my head. 'What're you doin' round here?' My dreams had already given that picture from earlier a good smash, had shattered it, so it wasn't throwing up details other than eyes. I was recovering. I couldn't any longer properly invoke the figure which had totally buckled the twilight. It must be like this.

'I . . .' My voice was stammering. 'I'm looking . . .' The kid narrowed his eyes. 'Where's the street?' It would just take a specific time period to put images like these through the erasing process.

'Have you any money, mister?' the kid said. 'Give us somethin'?'

I came out with: 'No.' His tiny eyebrows got cross.

'I'll scream,' he said. He looked right up at me and grinned. 'And then you'll be for it.'

'Look,' I said. The distance let out a small yell. I jerked. I started to walk back towards the alley. He picked up his skateboard and walked with me.

'Go on,' he said. I stopped again and turned. His finger was still at that cut. I was looking all around. 'Would you?' he asked me. I took out my wallet. The only cash I had was emergency cash. My hands were twittering.

'I don't have much,' I whispered and I handed him these two colourful tiny flags. This was special money. Money for dreams. His miniature hand touched my fingers. It was a warm mouse.

'Buddy!' There still was nobody in the night. He folded the money away tightly into his jeans pocket. 'You're fuckin' rich,' he laughed with his eyes bright.

'I don't work,' I told him. He dropped his jaw in a playful way. 'How do I get out of here?'

'Through there.' He waved his hand timidly at the alley.

'Thanks,' I said. I started walking. He skated with me. 'Thanks for showing me the way out.'

'It's cool,' he smiled. 'Where d'you live?' he asked.

I said, 'I appreciate it.' He giggled nervously. Then I turned quickly away down the alley. I was upside down.

'Thanks, mister!' he shouted out.

I walked rapidly up Hardwicke Street. A burglar alarm started up, wrapping an everlasting steel chain round the streets. This Earth we live on was right then unstable, I wanted to get indoors, away from violent stars. I came up towards the big street where this Maureen does her sucking. Smoke was rising from a rubbish pile, it was sighing, the street was trying to enchant itself. I had glittering garbage inside me and tart smoke from burning cardboard. It would just take time, I was thinking to myself. I can't cope until I can grasp what those eyes earlier signified for sure. Soon I will get it clear. Then I'll cope. My inside dream mechanism had done its best with them. It even now was working, I knew, to crush that image, to grind it right down to a substance as tender as petals. But it needed time. It would keep on at it till there was fat and blood on the cogwheels, till the boy at the wall with milky hair and whispery eyelashes was mangled to pure tears. I'll be able to cope with it soon, when piss and juice and the sweat between his sweet dirty arse have cooled off the situation here inside me. It just needs patience.

STORIES AT EL HAJEB AND S

———————

I HAD TO SIT DOWN. I had to dream, my head was full of too much light. I didn't think about my shorts for a moment. There was a tea stall with careless white tiling round it. I looked for a waiter. Just the night before I'd woken with a little scream. God knows why. I spent my whole time in El Hajeb shocked only at how like the brochure it was, and unhappy too about what had to be some lack in myself. Dreams of a girl were just beginning to kill the smell of dung when from behind me a voice croaked in a language I did recognize: 'You gotta watch those legs round here, they could end up in a kebab.' I looked round.

Neat beard, peaked cap, blacked-out glasses, maybe thirty-five-ish, head back against the tiles and rapidly liquescing. It was the sandals betrayed me, I was to find out later – he'd spied *Clarks* carved on the sole of one that rested on the knee of the other and made a guess: 'You English?'

'Well . . .' I focused my tongue – it could have been the first real word I'd moulded in six, seven weeks. 'Nearly.' He asked could he join me. An old man grinned and made specs with his fingers. I slid my camera to the edge of my table. He raised his arm, said, 'You're like me, you have that Scandinavian-type complexion,' and pointed at my face with a stump. I tried to cover my surprise but it was hot . . . it was hard to think . . . 'That's a bad hand you have,' was all I could manage.

'Cut it off myself,' he said with good humour. 'Few years ago.'

I wasn't sure if he was boasting. Without reacting, I called over the boy waiter. He came and stood beside us. He was flickering his eyes or something. I ordered us glasses of what I'd recently learned to call *thé noir avec du lait*. Those eyes wouldn't stop flickering and now I was sorry I'd called him. My neck was clamped. I could only pretend I hadn't looked up at the boy while this guy ordered a tagine. He chewed the word 'tagine'. The boy went off. Men in jeans were selling kaftans in the passage.

'Gangrene?' I resumed, trying to sound casual.

'Oh, nothing that exciting.' He glanced behind him. 'Just got bored with the stupid thing.'

I nodded to hide that I was swallowing. 'You're not serious.'

There was thought on his brow. 'I'm not serious.'

I was thrown for a moment and didn't hear everything he was saying. I was staring at that arm on the table and a fly on his eyebrow. Eventually I managed to listen. He called himself Tom. At the start of the year he'd left the US navy and had soon commenced a world trip anticipated eight and planned four years before. He'd flown San Francisco to the East Coast, London–Madrid, taken the train to Tangier; then it was autocars, a lift and a peak-season camel ride to this stony mirage he still sat in now. It was October and he had pastel-filtered and April-perfumed memories of his own voice. 'You must love it here,' I said, lazier than sarcastic. 'What do you do all day?'

'Love it?' He picked off his shades, looked to the side, spoke low. 'The flag in this town is flying upside down, you know. That's a nautical distress signal!'

I only had presumptions about sailors and I tried losing them as he talked. He was educated, apologised for shouting over the constant *fremitus*, was urbane, nourished a fantasy of publishing a book of postcards he'd written, then not posted, from every place he'd ever been. He rambled through farflung themes, even evoked the image of Alexander weeping when he'd nowhere else in the known world to conquer. Where was I on nationalism? The one good thing about Manila was you could get whatever you wanted to eat – grits, fried okra, black-eyed peas, anything, little wafers of lava, monkeys' eyelashes ... Did I read poetry? Was there an obligation on modern man to disrespect a person for loving him? I was half listening to it all while I watched girls swaying past with trays of biscuits on their heads. Since I'd been here languor and my own smell had returned me to the body I'd shed around fourteen, fifteen. I was alive, stickily so, and happy enough to rest there in the baked-in shadows. Till he asked me another question with genuine eyes. What was my most hellish adventure? Now he was putting me on the spot. I responded rebelliously: there were no more adventures to be had.

'No?' He looked along his nose.

I hadn't meant this seriously and I was almost glad that the boy returned with mint tea and no milk, flickering and muttering that a beautiful tagine would appear. Tom gave a starved grunt. The boy went off.

'Do you like mint tea?'

I said, 'Mad about it.'

But he hadn't mislaid our topic. 'So why can't we have adventures today? Forgive me, I'm probably stupid.'

My brain was nearly full up now. But suddenly I had a conviction and I was thoroughly organising my argument. There was dust on the skin of my tea. I began with LA one summer where I said my sister worked as a nurse. From there I flew to Laos. As I patchily made this up it started to sound like the sort of anecdote I thought he'd like. I get there, I feel really freaked and way out in the dusty East till I see an old European bloke in the hostel who speaks something like Dutch and I feel a bit more at ease. He introduces himself to me in a lisping, twangy English. I think: Christ, I'm not so far away at all. We get talking, I tell him where I came from. Then he says, 'Yes! I know Newtowncun-ningham. *The Hungry Spoon!*'

'No,' said Tom. 'What's the place called again?'

I realized I'd been enjoying a grin when it evaporated now. Kids stood gazing through us in a shared daydream. I commented vaguely about there being nowhere different in the world and he puzzled at distant green roofs. Prayers had started blowing from a minaret. Then the boy walked up again. He stood beside us. Tom nodded. The boy set down a dish. It was a burger. Tom's chin quivered.

I didn't say anything. It was a handsome enough burger but Tom was looking childish with a big bottom lip. A gap appeared between us while I rested my eyes and listened to the noise and had a dreamy image of Allah like an Arab despot praying. At last Tom leaned forward with a wicked glint, confidential mouth: 'Corporal, I can't go on any more. Set the town to the torch.' I was about to give a polite laugh when he stood up. 'Very nice meeting you. Forgive me, I've a bag to pack.' He gripped my hand. Curious, and strangely satisfied, I noticed he had a hard-on. As soon as he walked off I began to dream.

The following evening I walked into the new part of town that was freckled with oil stains and smelled of closing time. There was an empty blue everywhere – it was bluing lorries, it was on the faces of some dark kids who were standing about with a Sanyo box. Another was chasing a man up the pavement. On a cobbled corner across the boulevard was a café called, confusingly, Pourquoi Pat. I was afloat on the heat, needed a drink. I went in. It was at the counter I heard that voice.

'Well!'

I turned round.

'You're still here,' I said, I was thinking aloud. Tom was sitting with a glass of beer and a bitten roll.

I got my drink and joined him. Already I'd formed the clear

intention of probing him to see how he liked being put on the spot.

'I'm just not serious about this world trip,' he sighed. 'I've had too much already.'

'So why stay?'

He said he'd been meaning to move on for weeks, but it was easy to stay – yesterday he'd simply cancelled Dakar. He was taking stock, trying to think of something worth wanting in life. If I was interested he could explain. 'It's okay, you don't have to approve. To tell you the truth, well, I found all I was really looking for in Marrakech. Is that disgusting?' At his age, he went on, he was beginning to realize his life's purpose was pathetic, but at least now he knew what it was: he only wanted sex. He used to have some dim sense of cause when he'd found it difficult to get. And he laughed: 'Goddamn.' I ordered him another beer. The waiter eyed my shorts. Tom began to drink privately. I tried to start him up again. 'So there's nowhere left in the world any more?'

'I just don't like the world any more.'

I tried again: 'Wasn't Manila exciting?' He just shrugged. 'What was it like?'

'I swear I could bore you numb.' Outside camp palm trees were fluttering.

'No.'

He made thoughtful nods, then, sliding his grip up and down his glass without shame, he spoke. I took out a little knife and whittled my fingernails, but I was listening carefully, noting everything. His dad had been a diplomat, he'd been brought up there in a villa in suburbia with a dog and a cat and a monstrous moth that lived a year on the front wall. Their maid had been a real steaming nympho and he felt sure he lost his virginity at the age of five. Then two decades later his ship docked in Olongapo. On liberty at weekends he'd take the train to another Manila, but just as familiar: it really was all one big honkytonk district where the Ugly People lived, all called 'Joe' and 'Honey Ko' by the dusky girls and it didn't matter one bit they were oversized dorks, it was *peso*nality counted. I said weren't the Philippines just Hollywood and Coke, wasn't everywhere that? But he said, 'Understand, in Manila ads are the real thing!' He'd just had to withdraw to a bar off del Pelar that, typically, had taken its logo illegally from a famous one in Hong Kong. There in the brown mood of an afternoon, while kids came in to play Street Fighter II, he'd write about the soul-withering Far East on postcards, more like memoirs for himself than messages to another. 'Let me give you a detail a buddy of mine told me. Postcard from Manila. You see a small kid carrying a short-fused chicken. You go up to him. You tell him you'll give him five pesos if he bites the head off the chicken. You know he will. But you still don't feel any emotion.'

'What do you mean memoirs?' I asked so he knew he wasn't shocking me. But he was pleased and intimate.

'Well, my idea was . . . you know corny travel writing?' He did puzzled excitement: 'Why not do it in rhyme? I figure, what the hell, go the whole way. I call them postcards, but . . .' He knew a few snatches by heart. And soon I could see these places from their postcards. A bit was quite memorable, when he talked about the stuff he himself remembered best. It was something like:

> 'Recollect too well that counterfeit
> Stoned Crow in Manila; can never forget
> That zimmed tycoon amateur
> Of boys I met in Singapore'

It went on in that vein. I thought I'd better say, 'You should publish.' He hid a sigh like a nervous butterfly and stared at me. Then he raised his hand and placed it on my cheek.

'Don't worry.' He dropped it. 'Your complexion, that's all, it's interesting. Another beer?'

At that moment a beggar woman came into the café and he faked surprise. So she sat down at our table. She had had a sleeveless dress the colour of chocolate. And only one arm. I went tense. She smelled. Tom put a face on like someone trapped behind a casual look and stared out the window. She nodded at him. The finger-nails of her one hand were painted. He could only crack a joke: it was useful to do without a hand, at least this way you always have something to want. Just to get rid of the next silence I was about to ask this woman how she painted her nails when she took his hand. He jumped. She scratched his palm with a finger. 'L'hôtel?' she said to him, raising her eyebrows twice. The heat drained down my legs. 'You don't know that Chinese curse,' he spluttered, trying to ignore her, *I hope you get your wish!*' Across the street a waiter was taking tables and chairs in from the pavement. I just didn't know what to do. I was so self-conscious I decided I would take a holiday snapshot of her. 'Devastating idea,' he was saying, 'don't you think? No? Have you lost your voice?'

But all of a sudden I'd realized I hadn't my camera with me. I couldn't remember when I had it last. The woman winked at him. 'Oh God, she really likes me.' He took his hand from hers.

'My camera,' I said weakly. 'I don't know where it is.' He rested his stump on the table. The woman looked repulsed. 'I've lost it,' I mumbled. I was stunned. I'd lost some great Third World clichés, the skimpy purpose this place had given me. With an unfunny laugh he said, 'The waiter stole it, of course – just a regular snafu,' like he was pouring warm beer over my picture of it sitting on the table of the tea stall the afternoon before. The woman finally gave up on us. Making out to be blasé, she took his roll and went to some Arab men at a table at the back. 'I'm sure if you lost your postcards,' I said, 'you'd be just as casual.'

'I'd die.'

'Yeah.'

'Anything wrong with that?'

'Maybe's there's a lot wrong with it,' I muttered.

He gave a loud sigh to calm himself and gripped his glass. 'Maybe you don't know what you're talking about.'

'Me?' I pretended outrage to play for time. 'You're claiming to know the world. But maybe you just won't let go of your Western middle-class culture?' I was surprised how suddenly we'd got to this point, and frustrated to hear my dusty words: 'Only they could believe your fake internationalism, I suppose.' I showed an innocent smile.

'Explain that,' he said, concentrating.

I knew I couldn't. I wasn't settled and I was too absorbed in hoping the woman would leave the café. 'Well,' I sighed, 'obviously, it's that body-denying thing.'

'Body-denying.'

I was confused myself. 'The middle class,' I tried again, 'has the same tastes everywhere. International culture, where's the diversity there?' I began to bluff confidence but my voice was wobbling. 'I mean, the original differences are still in the lower classes. They've no mobility, they embody locality. But it's like difference isn't official. But that's culture alive ...' He was listening hard. 'As opposed to ... middle-class denial of the body. And never at rest. Living in ... expectation ... I don't know what I'm talking about!'

That appealed to him. He chuckled and leaned towards me. 'What I like about you,' he confided, fingering his eye, 'is I think you could despise me.' He continued to chuckle.

We had to get out of the café. Strolling through the flavoured smokes and fragrances of pollen and petrol we calmed down. A man was sweeping the tipsy boulevard with a palm leaf. A kid with a pillow-pink rash staggered past him and kicked his pile of squashed cockroaches. Tom was renting an apartment over a garage where a Pegasus flickered and Mobil Oil was on sale. He suggested we carry on talking over some dirty gin if I was into it.

'Sure.' I'd a feeling we were going to make fools of ourselves. Which was the only adventure going in this town.

He chased two slippery boys out of his stairway who'd probably been making love. Up in the apartment there were roaches on the walls. And with the window open to a perfect big blue that tireless cicadas snipped at, we sat close and drank that gin. Or rather he drank it, I couldn't get that dirty idea off my tongue. But I was beginning to feel better. We laughed a bit. Then he asked to borrow my sarcastic ear and gave a humorous account of his world trip so far complete with rolling eyes, dispirited voice, striped and dotted perils. I wanted to remember it. I was so intent I didn't even twig for a while that when he was most evocative he was talking again in rhyme, reciting a recent postcard. 'My name on a cheque sorta granted me a wish,' he said. 'Swooped me to the hot slanted adobe, the wan flat tops, verandas and tumbledown highrise of Casablanca. But further south I sensed that wish.' He switched on his fan. I took an olive, relishing the comfort. He was getting stagier. And drunker. 'Rubbed a genie in Marrakech up the wrong way. Got love. Too much. More than I'd dreamed of ...' Trying to remember, he halted me with his hand. So I spoke, anxious to be sarcastic.

'Love, yes, I've heard of that.'

But he was soon reciting again, and I found I was hearing sounds more than sense — love among lunacy, envious stumps, orange noon's dazzle on dazzle in orange groves ... And he was looking sadder. 'And naked? Yeah. Too much of that. I couldn't take it. All I could want I got. And more.' He spilled some gin. 'Now what can I hope for?'

I gave him a respectful silence and then said, with only a trace of boredom, 'You're a poet.' He leaned close. That stump went on my knee. A crazy idea suddenly came to me to wait to see if I could possibly get a hard-on at that; but after a moment he was knocking it on his cheek.

Outside wasn't getting any brighter. He offered to make coffee. When he was in the toilet I sneaked out the door and started back along a field of pylons and quivering elephant grass to my hotel. I was so wound up I was rushing. Seeds were all over the road.

I'd had enough of Tom and his stories. The next morning I sat in the old part of town far below the sky, trying to drink tea made in hot milk that wouldn't cool. I still hadn't relaxed. Everything seemed distant and beige. Men on the passage were perhaps weaving cheap magic into carpets. I tried to read the headlines in a tourist's newspaper – goose steps all across Germany? Italy breaking up? I didn't feel safe. Maybe I was unwell. Kids wound through the tables selling mirrors encased in yellow metal or just came up and took the sugar lumps. As I thought about them two words – 'spiritual junk' – came together in my head with a picture of God in a black shirt. A waiter brought croissants and I ate one in front of a kid with flat cheeks that met like the prow of a boat and shocking black hair and full lips. I was only relieved it didn't upset me. And a wisecrack came to me, I should have used it with Tom in the Pourquoi Pat: you always felt more sad at these details when you saw them in Sunday supplements. The kid went begging round the other tables with a tree and its poster of Hassan II in his background. I couldn't stop thinking: it was obvious I wasn't stunned at all that I'd lost my camera, there was just no way of capturing anything new. I was only amazed that photography could bore me now – after all, it had for so long seemed to me no less than a way of illustrating my life! I got up and gave my remaining croissant to the kid who snatched my hand and kissed it and guzzled and ran away now with balloon cheeks. I walked back to the hotel to lie down.

Some time later I woke with a shout. It was a struggle to remember where I was. The bed was damp. I swung off it. There was a rusty tap in my room that spurted coloured waters, so I cooled myself all over. I had a muddled anxiety that overnight the West's credibility had perished. Twilight leaked through the shutters. I lay back and tried to clear my head. I didn't even know what the West meant, I only had scraps of ideas I didn't quite believe: we were somehow unnatural, living vicariously, our taboo about the moment . . . imperialism . . . images . . . Kids were squealing outside and a football was thudding.

The next morning I disappointed myself. I walked over to Tom's apartment. His district was all dove-greys of abandoned lorries in the heat. You couldn't buzz up to him so I stood hesitating outside. A man in uniform was dozing on a doorstep. It wasn't certain Tom would be here. He had at one point started disparaging Sierra Leone; he wasn't sure if he should get an early coach up north to redeem his ticket, then come back. Or maybe he'd moved on after all. Which was his window, I wondered. Paint was peeled off the façade in obese patches.

I went into the building and up the stairs. Behind the door of his apartment there were movements. I knocked. He was neatening his beard when he answered. 'A thousand good mornings,' he said heavily, staring at my legs. I wandered to the window and he fiddled about. In the far distance a lifeless hotel with a flat top stood facing the sky.

'Lovely apartment. Did I say that?'

'Probably.' He was on edge. He took his passport. We went out.

We didn't know what to do as we walked. A donkey loaded down with hi-fi stuff was tied to a telegraph pole. I said we could either just walk or view trees or go to the souks again and buy cards. We just walked (*parlambled*, as he called it). When we heard some thuds we stopped and looked in a doorway. A man was chopping bones. We stood and watched him. 'Chopping bones,' I said emptily.

'Nice.' His stump was in his pocket.

We walked on without talking. When our legs clapped out we were on a lane of empty garages with some bags of grain against a wall. A fly kept returning to my finger. We sat down on the bags. Two boys were throwing a kitten to each other. 'So,' I said. I tried to get something to say. 'So.'

'Right.'

His reticence was depressing me. I muttered, 'I could really hate that fly.' He didn't react. I tried to think up a question he'd have to answer and a moment later I tossed one: 'Where do you think really is different? Is there anywhere?'

His words were so tired of irony he could only just budge them off his tongue. 'Well, I could give you the gist of my China postcard?'

'Do.'

'A story to help fill the void?'

'Yeah.'

He smirked at himself. 'I gotta be, I mean, what's it all . . .? Oh, don't ask. My way of coping . . .'

'Go for it.' I disowned my T-shirt and settled to listen. He stared through me for some moments before beginning.

Tom is spending a year in Berlin. In the summer he takes the Trans-Siberian express. Ten days across flat waste peel away layers of protection. He sets sail from Vladivostok. On the deck he sees a European woman. He needs to talk. It's the East or nothing now, he blurts out and she turns round. She likes this kind of talk. By the time London had become a hell a great *taedium vitae* had overwhelmed the West . . . It's true, she says. She's on a cultural exchange from Berlin. He'd never met her there. Now he meets her on the boat to China. He wonders, could it be meant? We are making sunburst love on the Yellow Sea, she marvels, the world must have brought us together, somehow, by winds and waves, invisible currents . . .

I was involved in what Tom was saying till I noticed he had his hand on his balls. It stayed there as he carried on about this woman. How she seems to have a thin German personality, but she's only thin till you walk round her.

'Yeah?'

'Yeah,' he said and, without looking at me, he pulled his zip down. 'Then,' he laughed, 'she's into Adolphe Appia. She dotes on her pathetic father's ghost – some "undiscovered genius".' And he winkled his cock out.

My eyes looked round to see if we were being watched. The boys weren't noticing. I didn't know what was going on but I nodded as he rubbed himself and talked. On the boat they're getting high on romantic ideas, such a joke – they think they could have this great bond. Let us test the coincidence of our encounter, she says. They choose a task: to meet one evening at the same address in Beijing.

I was sitting on a knife – was Tom not clear what country he was in? He was glancing around and still trying to get a hard-on. 'I mean, picture it. China. You can't read street signs. Maps. Can't ask directions. Will they have public transport?' His voice was getting slighter as he explained. 'Remember, nobody's ever seen a Caucasian, all they'll do is gawp. Like you're from Neptune or . . .' He stared at his limp hard-on. When he spoke again he was quavering. 'Well, I take the train to Beijing. It's a cinch, I get a taxi downtown. Careen through all the smell of shit and spices. Voices, horns blowing. Amazing place. Atop some street we screech to a halt. There it is. I'm early.' He swallowed. At last he put it away. 'She calls my name from a high window.' Now he looked straight at me with twitchy cheeks. 'On the way up the stairs I think: look, it worked. I have my China postcard.

Chrissakes, I don't want to make love to this woman! I go back down and out on to the street.'

The two boys now were sitting on the pavement. 'That was an extraordinary story,' I said. His eyes fell on his elbow.

I got to my feet. I didn't know what to do. It was getting even hotter. I was wishing I could just somehow sidle off when he murmured, looking at a long wall, 'This place isn't good for us.' The kitten at the boys' feet yawned.

It was time for me to leave anyway and over the next week I told myself I was going to get a train back home; but I lingered like some lengthy yawning shadow. One afternoon was packed with bleating but there was no explanation to be seen. Some girls were collecting for a cat and its kittens. I grew fond of watching the *pieds noirs* types, one in a blond button-thru dress faltering about on crutches looking peachy and tormented. By now my head was spiced up with weird ideas: we were, all of us, like tourist attractions for visiting angels. Did God hate, or just not feel? It was okay if he didn't feel – I couldn't feel for here any more than I could cry at the news, I thought. But my hands were trembling. I didn't know what state I was in. I was strangely relaxed. I seemed to have shed an old burdensome anxiety to build up some decorative identity for myself; and that scared me.

And then I spotted Tom doodling near the souks. A waiter was sprinkling water over his feet. I approached him from behind. 'Still here,' I reassured him and sat down.

Without looking at me he said, 'I could cut Liberia?'

'Mmm,' was all that came out of my mouth. A stone was sitting between his knife and fork. I didn't look at it in case he'd put it there. 'I suppose you could.'

'You're right, I could.'

The next morning we left El Hajeb, but only to go further south. We got up before light and tiptoed to the bus station. He had a dedicated grin. 'You might pick up a great souvenir down here. Like maybe a phial of crushed rhinoceros horn. To get you horny.' We boarded a coach as morning ripened with yellows and shadows like a bruised banana. I didn't regret it: from the windows I saw that documentary horror image of sheet-metal abodes along a railway line, but sunned on, infested with smiles. 'Look, about the other day, I . . .' Tom's head dropped close as we rattled on. 'I was just a bit depressed. But it was sick.' There was an old man towing a mule, a delicate wave. 'Assuming you didn't like it, of course?' I crossed my legs.

We skirted the Atlas Mountains where there were goats in a tree. By about noon we'd no more bottles of water. Even the coach gave a splutter. I watched for cracks to appear in Tom's cheeks. He said if the worst happened we could always suck on a cactus, look under a stone, burble spells. And the next moment we went microscopic. There began a level immensity of unloved world. Later I pointed out a mirage: a BP rig had an outlying housing estate, TV aerials, birds on telegraph wires. 'I'm beginning to think you might be cynical,' he said. From stupor we awoke hours later among powder-puff walls in late evening and oily faces agog. Drums clattered. Cornets wailed. The local feculence rose to greet us. When we stepped down and out someone slammed a sun on our backs. Together we managed it across a sandy square to a doorway, nudged it off us, stumbled in. It was Africa.

It really was as real as TV Africa. It was some little dot we knew began with S. We would have despised it but the sun had freckled all our feelings. Days overlapped like shadows, nights were bunged with the dark uproar of the bazaar. In the mornings we'd make it to the cactus garden behind the boarding house we stayed in and sit with a parasol between us and the sizzling blue. Chameleons sat on the low bordering wall casting stares. Tom was constantly amused and drunk. When he talked he stared through snake charmers, storytellers, madmen on the square, ignoring them. To him now *The City* was the only place on Earth to be. As he spoke his eyes followed memories playing among the opuntias: California Street . . . I had to visit him . . . Harry's — *a crummy sandwich bar on van Ness and Ellis* . . . I knew if I spoke I'd quarrel because I was trying to form ideas, make sentences in my head. How could we find the ambition to go home now? I hadn't even the will to get up and buy Levis from a stall to cover my legs. Home to me was just a place somewhere where I'd collected shots and souvenirs of other places. There was a story there for him to think about. But my head was too dizzy. My legs blistered. 'Title: *Postcards from Hell*. What do you think? A bit over-the-top?'

I found myself trying to explain a day or two later. We were both annoyed at the bad idea for an omelette we'd eaten. He was sitting crushing miniature writing on to postcards he'd bought in some passageway. A toddler in a dress was watching us from outside the garden. I was waiting for the moment when I knew he'd lay his pen down and say, 'Is your ear busy?' I didn't react. The toddler had started winking. I gave a brief dull laugh, I couldn't help it. I was weird. I was a shard of glass glinting in the sun. 'That's kind of you,' he said, and started reading. There were some men eating to one side of us and they tried to follow it. It was full of the same sentiments. I took out my knife and nipped the table. I only listened to a few lines.

> 'No explorer. Call me intrepid collector
> Of breakneck fancies: is my nightmare Dakar
> But Nigeria's shadow, was blood on the Congo
> The bit I missed most four weeks ago?'

When at last he stopped I didn't even breathe.
'You don't like it?'
'Oh is it over?'
'Well?'
'It's great,' I answered. 'I don't know.'

He lifted his pen with a smile. 'You don't know what?'

I was growing impatient. 'I'm sorry?' I said.

'So you've something to say, spit it out.'

'What have I to say?'

'I'd like to hear your argument.' I didn't answer. A chameleon shot out its tongue. 'If you think you could express it?'

'Oh I think so.' He folded his arms. He adjusted his chair. 'Well what's the point, that's all.' He looked over at the toddler. She hurried a nod.

'The point?'

I made a real effort. 'These stories,' I said. 'Creating form . . . I mean, out here it's real. Just sand and sun and the moment. But we're afraid to feel alive, aren't we? We have to sublimate that. We'd rather reject experience, build something clean and pretty. Keep postponing, you know . . .'

'I know I'm repressed. Is that what you're trying to say?'

I jabbed my knife right in the table. He looked at it. 'I don't know,' I said. I swallowed unpleasantly. 'It's just . . . I don't know.' Beyond the square the medina was a hill of broken walls, fragile turrets, washing lines. 'I don't know.'

He yawned. 'Oh really.'

I was instantly furious.

'What's that supposed to mean?' When he only shook his head it made me madder. 'I think that just *sounds* like it means something. What does "Oh really" mean? I think it means you can't think of a reply.'

'I mean, "Oh really",' he said, examining his stump with contempt.

Now I couldn't think what to say myself. All I could do was nod and sigh putridly, 'I see.'

He stared at me for maybe half a minute. Until, all at once, his hand was round my throat.

I couldn't breathe. His eye was right against mine. But, just as quickly, he released me. He laughed nervously. The men at the other table began to jeer at him – 'Ali Baba! Hé! Touriste!' As he dusted down my T-shirt I tried to recover some dignity.

'Yeah,' I grinned, but I was in pain. 'You might be an asshole, but I've got to admire your style.'

He smiled unsurely. He leaned forward.

'What you need is relief,' he said. 'I can see it on your face. I'm not talking about sincerity, trust. Just think of me as a machine.'

I got up to go. 'Tell me something,' I said. 'I've always wanted to know.' Now I wanted to be crushing. But I withered at what came out of my mouth. 'How are you able to tie your shoe laces?' I could only turn away with pretended confidence. The toddler walked after me milking my finger.

That evening I couldn't stand my own company. I wore out my Clarks logo going up and down the few pink streets like a zonked-out Perseus looking for Tom. A kid with broken legs bumped himself after me. Women wailed. The desert seemed to be blowing closer across the sky. I couldn't find him and ended up going to my room. There I couldn't doze – the drums and shouts below I didn't mind by now; worse was that sound Tom liked to call *fritinancy*, like insects nibbling your head. The bed slowly began to sway and still my mind wanted to clarify my argument with him, rehearse it. Wasn't he living solely to write a good autobiography? That was so shallow. I pictured my words shocking his face as it recognized the truth. 'But you've never lived. It's like me living for photography: *I was here!* Ha! So what?' I laughed and realized with a shock that I was chattering out loud. Now I was on my feet and puking flagrantly over the walls. Before I lay back again I was asleep . . .

The room, when I woke, was a cube of light. There was a faraway thumping in my head. My hair was sore. I remembered a vivid dream. Tom and I had been joking and he'd said, 'What would really humiliate me, what would be too embarrassing?' As we were laughing he took all his clothes off. He got down on his belly on the dust. He pushed himself forward giggling, 'Insect, insect. Is this embarrassing?'

I lifted my head a little, sensing Tom's voice. There was thumping at the door. 'I'm coming in!' I heard now. 'Holy . . .!' He was in the doorway gaping at me. 'I thought you'd gone already.'

'What?'

'You were screaming. You know that?'

There were bright dots of puke all over the room, my baggage was scattered on the floor. And I stank. For the next few days I wove in and out of speckled dazes. Tom stayed nearby and that blew out Mombasa–Bombay. He cleaned up, brought me water, tried some powder or something on my forehead. Then one day he was entertaining me. I lay on my front with the white strips from the shutters grilling my eyes. He figured I should be better by now. I tensed as he let his hand fall on my thigh 'Does the master wish I give him a massage?' I lay and tried to imagine how unpleasant this would be. His shadow covered the floor.

'Don't care,' I mumbled into the pillow.

He gently lifted my leg. What I had was really depression, he said softly. We both had that terrible one only the sun could induce. He'd heard of it. Now he was feeling it. We'd given up, we couldn't go on. 'You want to know what it is?' he whispered, and he made his voice go sickened. 'The cafard!' He was off again. I reluctantly listened: the French Foreign Legion had gotten it, just weren't used to the African heat, gave up on life, then sickness came, they would never fight, were sitting ducks . . . His voice had got hoarser. 'God help us resist the cafard. Cafard lost Dien Bien Phu and Algeria. Is that helping?' The bed creaked.

'It's horrible.'

35

'Oh.'

'You can go if you want. Please.'

But his warm hand began to circle my arse. 'Why don't I make you feel really disgusting?' he said kindly.

A silence followed and for no reason at all I saw seeds blowing on a pavement at evening. I grunted, 'Okay.'

He didn't speak for a minute. Then he cleared his voice. 'Oh well, if you must be sarcastic . . .' He walked out of the room.

The next morning I appeared for liquid. The weather had changed. Palms were flapping against a dull warm sky. I sat down, ordered tea. A new waiter was growing a delicious grape under his ear. Tom had a bottle of deserty wine of what had to be cactuses and pink horizons. His lips were moving. I ignored him. A glass of cold milk and a Lipton's teabag came. Tom mumbled, amused, 'Blew a whole world trip. Imagine'. The muezzin started. It whipped up dust and his postcards scattered off the table. They lifted themselves over the garden. He refused to notice. I buttoned up my shirt. 'Never get another chance,' he said.

I saw an opportunity to throw back his words, but I was so weak I was almost miming: 'Oh really.' He thought for a second. I felt a raindrop.

'Why don't I just walk out into the desert and not come back?' He waited for an answer. 'You think I wouldn't?' A cardboard box was hopping across the square. 'Is that it?' He leaned on his elbows. 'I think that's what this guy would like to say. But has he got the wherewithal?' Now my feet were getting damp. He stared at me closely. 'You think I'm a bullshitter.' All of a sudden the rain came pelting down. 'Don't even think it!'

'Oh.'

'Oh is right.'

'Definitely.'

'You better believe it.'

I didn't move. He stood up. He walked out of the garden in the downpour and across the square. I dashed inside. There were bubbles on the ground.

Late that night I woke with cold balls. He whispered, 'We're going home.' I rolled onto my front. 'Tomorrow.'

'You came back.'

'Well, I . . .' He was breathing fire.

'Not a bullshitter?'

'Yeah, so what?' His face came closer. 'You know I'm just a bit of garbage.' His sigh stuttered. He was kneeling on the contents of my suitcase. Suddenly, he kissed me. And now I began to fume.

'Oh yeah!' I could barely catch my breath to speak. 'You know . . . it seems to me you think . . .' I was trying hard to order my thoughts. I sat up. 'I'll tell you, will I?' It was my chance to get everything across I'd been thinking, but I was weak and it was coming to me in too great a rush. 'You're boring, that's all. You're ordinary.' He grinned and blinked. 'Pretending to despair – for the thrill. That's it. The ultimate postcard: *Abandoning world trip – the cafard*. Oh sure!' I tried to sound cocky, but I was shocked to find tears coming to my eyes. It surprised him. 'You just can't stop. But I lost all that crap. I can't believe in any of it any more. I've lost everything.' As words spilled from me I was sobbing now. 'Let's die here then . . . real, not just a postcard . . . storytelling, addicted to it . . . and isn't it really not being able to show love?'

As I paused he bit on a finger. A silence was singing in the room. I cleared my eyes and began again. But I was lost in anger. '. . . afraid to be ordinary . . . think you're Albert Camus? . . . you love yourself. Kill yourself? Ha! you're too chicken . . . What an act!' His hand hesitated. My knife was sitting on the table. '. . . can't tell the truth . . . so you won't have to feel . . . But God doesn't write poetry, did you think of that? . . .' I was soon bawling things I didn't understand. He was looking all over the room, it was spinning and I was soaked in sweat. 'Fascist! How did you really lose that hand? *So worthless and wretched* – shit! You mean so poetic and dignified . . . think you're God? Say something!' His stump was waving around now. 'How much do you hate yourself? That's the test. What can you say to that! Nothing? Well? Bourgeois . . . aristocrat . . . postcard . . . bullshitter . . .'

But I could see that his movements were becoming certain. His wrists were on his waist. Now, he was letting out a noise. And when I heard it I stared at him horrified for the first time. He was flapping his arms and making a chicken sound. I froze on the bed. He danced around the room with his tongue wagging out, it was too embarrassing. At long last he opened the door and noisily made off.

Before dawn I woke with a loud laugh. I sat up quickly. My sheets were soaked. I leaned back against the wall without thinking. At last I got dressed.

I left the hotel for some time and walked through the grey light and dusty winds to get the coach that passed by on the road twice a week in the early morning from Mauritania. Hours later the coach finally took over the galloping desert and was tortuously slow to stop beside me. So there it was.

When I got on the passengers twitched, a plump terra-cotta mother with kids and bags occupying half the coach, a sleeping couple and goat, a bald black guy who started drumming on the upholstery and a girl with a *Rough Guide* I almost thought I knew from back home. I wondered was I deliberately mad as I sat at the back and we took off. I could have been. Or was I being delivered from a clarity all around? From the mad certainty of a desert heading north across the sky. From a tyrannical light, now so gently wrapping blue around the paper collage huts of river people. But yes, there it was. I wanted to laugh and couldn't. My eyes were burnt out and my head was flickering with images –

for what it was worth I was in the end bringing back snapshots of the whole hilarious escapade: a dolled-up woman with an arm missing; one kid by a café with a deformed head and lips for kissing; a show of uncircumcised pallor on a sleeping Muslim street . . . We were shifting distance now as the road widened, hurtling away from a hundred absurd dinners, away from a million beggars and amputees, all of them blown to the pavements like a generous waste of seeds. But I was feeling nothing. Or perhaps a little colourful sentimentality? I was simply moving away. Away too, of course, from that entirely deceived guy, that victim I'd maybe underestimated, but who was nothing without his touched-up traveller's tales. Would I ever get those stories out of my head? That glossy one about a romance that dissolved when he thought there was nowhere exotic left in the world. How in this country he'd fulfilled his *most unutterable dreams* and paid the price for it when there was no reason any more to move on. But they couldn't compare to what I'd managed to tell him in the end: I'd had my eyes opened – he'd called it the cafard; either way, there was nothing left of our whole unnatural culture I could believe in. But neither was it crushing me any more. I cared about nothing. Nothing. But I wasn't afraid of living. Maybe I could love a little? At least I wasn't so much without hope that I had to live out these pointless, elaborate stories to feel like something. And he'd believed it all. It was a good one. A horrible one.

III

———————

GREY AREA

———————

THERE WAS COLOUR, I could not argue with that. Even though we languished in a Catholic ghetto in Belfast, even though what soon proved to lie beyond it was little other than the same burnt concrete, scrapmetal sky and sooty rain, and even though we failed throughout to get more than a distant glimpse of sex, it is true that at the end there was, uniquely, one delinquent wee splash – if I can refer in this way, without downplaying it, to an act of killing. Yet, to be frank, it was a matter of no great significance on that dirty white evening as it began to drizzle and Vomit's khaki jacket was flailing back at the bleached breeze and the light was going down over identical chimneys and cable lines of birds; indeed, it was at that last moment with even more than our usual stolidness that the three of us conceded that, yes, as things stood, we might as well murder. Since I should recount all the background facts from the beginning, let me make it clear that, apart from this brief more colourful, more favourable spell, all things were invariably one or another shade of grey. I have to begin by evoking the smoke-greyness of burning buses on our wet way to school while the depressed sun slept in. One such morning I shouted up ahead of me: 'Bleep!'

The streets were thronging with our charcoal-grey uniforms and I thought I could recognize a schoolmate of mine standing in an untidy gang each member of which stared pop-eyed and flummoxed down the road. 'Duffies!' It was purely by shape or size that I could tell a person from a distance, or very occasionally by the particular slogan on a canvas bag, each one vicious but none original. And while gender was a factor which played a part in differentiating us from girls, I was now about to observe that by far *their* most remarkable feature stood out on the greywash like a hope or a wish or a temptation – it was a struggle to define it.

'Look at that!' Bleep, who was occasionally known as Duffy and whose figure and dark complexion had to all appearances been squashed at some stage from above, spoke to me without turning when I drew up. Distantly, a sluggish cortège was dissolving into the curves of the cemetery wall. I stood for a moment thinking. The girls became the morning mist. Quite suddenly, he released a wolf whistle and the others started up with agitated, idiotic signals to the air. 'Hey, Mary Poppins!' they yelled.

In contrast to the life around me now, down there – even with umbrellas – an unabashed, not ungraceful quality expressed itself. I could tell that this recognition was causing me some interest by the sparkling in my lower torso. It was rough down the road, there it was ultimate ghettoland, a no-go zone, I had never wanted to go there; still, the distance seemed to throw back from long ago a delicate whirl of confusions. Bleep rummaged on the ground for projectiles and tossed them forward in simple bewilderment. I tried to concentrate in spite of him. Down there was the forgotten pleasure of carefree movement, I seemed to be remembering that rare encounter with the human body I had had on one or two occasions – I felt I was getting close as the gang now brayed and quacked like certified tubeheads – an encounter which had, in front of me, swept or twitched back into the world its fugitive colours. A hint of fullbloodedness was betraying itself here. Yes – I may have cracked it – at last I could acknowledge how much it was troubling me – my embarrassing peers were on

their toes flapping their hands and burbling, 'Look at her gloves!'
– that these girls' uniforms (if they were indeed female) were
distinctly, almost disloyally reddish.

Admittedly they were a dull red, you might say a grey-red, a
red as near to redlessness and black while still maintaining some
hope of red; but all the same, here was a lightness sufficient to
transform, to inflame what, after all, were merely swaying
haunches and swinging pigtails. The warmish shade had to
explain my interest because – and here I must stress the need to
cover all significant aspects of my story – it was not as though
girls themselves were unfamiliar to us. They played out on the
streets like us in denim suits. Very often girls stood as men
beside us boys. It was their toughness which we tried to emulate.
Karen Burns, to name only one, once beat up my best friend's
dad. They were physically intense like butchers or pylons. We
were jealous of their biceps. But now as we stood delaying,
unwilling for school and curious at those blushes on the smoke,
you could say that there stirred a new unformed knowledge of
something in the world that was distinct and living and, ridiculous
as it sounded, natural. 'It's five to nine, fuck it,' Bleep mumbled,
intruding into my reverie. We proceeded up the road with a
perceptibly quicker shuffle and came to the school gates after the
siren had sounded.

The hydra-headed vigilance of gate duty ensured this morning
that we would retain the right to boast of the school's most
dislocated ears. It was, as I hope will be recognized, no small
wonder that thoughts of murder came to us so young.

'Oh Christ,' Bleep sighed, pressing on his ear as we made for
the school building.

'What?'

'It's Tuesday.'

Some bureau-loving midnight malefactor was no doubt the cause of our having to endure first thing on a Tuesday morning most unlucky, nefarious double Latin. We were a tiny, rancorous, smarting protest for the Embryo – Mr Turner, Latin teacher, so-called because of his formidable age (he was so old he *looked* like an embryo).

'Oh Maguire-us! Wretche maxime!'

The class sneered damply.

'And . . . with the death most heroic,' I struggled, 'so shall the law' – in my pauses I could hear pages rustling – 'do nothing otherwise than' – a few hissers were not waiting for me to finish – 'climb.' He let out a deep squeak. I risked a glance up. He was fluttering his watery eyes. I made another guess: 'Wander?' As he cleared his lean throat, tendons sat out. 'Be?'

'Having been found treacherous to his clan,' that thin voice began to quaver, 'Maguire-us the Untrue shall now be sacrificed.' I gazed through the page. I had very little to give Latin. Each single one of my thoughts recognized that their first duty was to render powerless the worring mystery or psychology or aesthetics of girls' skirts. 'Maguire-us – altar *now*!' I stood up and clod-hopped through the schoolbags to the front of the class. 'When are you likely to learn, small dog,' he said, his fine white eyebrows trembling high above me, 'that Latin is not random like your mind?' He was genuinely weary. 'We have rules, Maguire-us, simple, logical, predictable.' The parts of his body wobbled. Everybody was waiting to hear what the logical consequences for me would be. 'Creature . . .' he began. There was full attention. 'Bucket!' A single honk sounded from the class. So, I took stock, it was the head-in-the-bucket routine, there was nothing more predictable. I advanced to the wastepaper bin and knelt on one knee. He looked expectant.

'All the way in, sir?'

'Utmost speed, canine.' I lowered my head into the bin to the applause of my peers. Banana skin, crisp packet, Fanta tin and a nostril-crumpling whiff was the godforsaken region into which I now descended. I cursed him darkly: *one day, Embryo, I'll pickle your swollen head, have you aborted, give you hell,* etc. At length, 'Maguire-us, sit,' tinnily reverberated and, retrieving my head from the rubbish, I grinned all the way back to my seat and the luxury of fresh classroom perspiration. 'At the neglect of homeworks there will be weeping and wailing and lamentation of mothers,' the crooning continued. 'Next, most warlike Duffius.'

'I haven't done it either, sir.'

'Duffius – bucket!'

I sometimes saw myself cast as Aeneas, escaping with great fortitude from the Cyclops in some vague old Technicolor film. But most of the time it was impossible to work up any respect for that incredible lot who, when personally instructed by gods, would storm forward in swollen obedience and restore all properness with magic spears. Few of us listened to the ageless Embryo screech about that world he remembered before Christ. We passed notes in class: 'Up the Ra' and 'I'll get you tarred and feathered, wee lad, right?' At last one day our disrespect dribbled out.

Bleep and I were among the boysweat and pimply bottoms of the school changing room, undressing side by side for the compulsory shower after Gym. This was a complex ritual which involved both modesty and discreet peeps by which vital comparisons were made, so it was confusing to be approached at that moment by the third idler from hated Latin, now dressed only in a towel – Vomit. He was dubbed so on account of his severe condition of desquamating skin which made everyone want to throw up at first sight of him. He had a suggestion.

'Get him fucked up.' He looked down at us, unable to disguise enthusiasm. 'Beamer has this secret phone number.'

Bleep deftly swept a towel around him. 'What're you talking

about?' He peered up fatly as Vomit, who was roughly twice his size, explained.

'You know the way the Embryo's really Irish and all?'

'Is he?' I chipped in.

'So?' Bleep hurried him.

'Well, look, Beamer has this number.'

We made our way to the cramped showering area to shamble in the nude like cattle being doused – farts, splashes, shivers, pissing on Podge and not a flaccid member to be seen. Even Podge's button hardened to a piece of clove rock. And as though privacy could be diminished further, Vomit persisted, 'What do you think?' winking as if he had proved himself at long last. I considered this shameful and painfully simple behaviour which it was charitable to pretend not to notice, and concentrated on obscuring myself in some fashion. So I was taken by surprise when Bleep answered.

'Yeah.'

'Get that bastard shot,' Vomit gloated. Bleep smiled. Obviously this was not his usual backfiring, overly elaborate effort to be accepted. I made out my hand was in a relaxed dangle over my groin while I tensed my brain for any drip of inspiration. There was a confidential phone number which everyone knew about and could use, or then again more sneaky and ingenious pranksters – though everyone knew this too – could ring up the Brits with farfetched stories about their noisy neighbours, sullen grandmothers. My imagination was doing no better than that when, all at once, the siren started up, as droning and meaningless as the Embryo himself.

'What number?' I asked as we hurried back into the changing room. 'Is he into the IRA or something?'

They gave no answer. We quickly dressed.

'How did Beamer get the number?' Bleep called across to Vomit as he tied a shoe.

'Probably where he lives,' Vomit answered squarely before we made our way out of the changing room, hastening slowly to another crazy double bill of our least favourite superhuman characters.

I was not at all clear what they had been saying, but it had to be interesting if we could bring about the real live death of the Embryo by some intricate deceit involving telephone calls, to slap the jowls of the farcical law and have our own justice *in personam*, you might say. Over the next few days at lunchtimes Bleep and Vomit came up with further suggestions. Although these were idle at first, it was not long before we were all plotting in a spirit of hilarious self-discipline. A momentum developed, we goaded each other on, producing ever finer points, choosing the best day to strike; we even dreamed about the scheme and came in the next morning with divinely ministered details. And finally, and at last, when we held under our gaze a strategy, perfect and monstrous and unwanted, a baffled and ugly thing independent now, with its own life and unlovable demands, there was one moment of embarrassment when we each agreed silently, without saying a word more, to ignore it. As for myself, the truth was that I had only sworn in dead earnest the whole time to prove to Dryface and Bouncy Ball Duffy in what depths of cynicism I could still thrive. But actually to do this deed, for me, would have been a brand new concept entirely. So, as before, typically, predictably, nothing happened; the status quo was endured. Until one Thursday at break Bleep came up to me by the lockers. We had just enjoyed his protracted and stammering distinction between *therefore* and *because of* from the waste bin.

'I'm gonna kill the Embryo,' he seethed. His eyes vitrified.

We laughed. But we arranged to meet after school to discuss alternatives to this onerous stoicism.

'The half-lamppost?'

'Aye.'

The half-lamppost was our meeting place according to custom. Consistently, diminutive kids made thwarted efforts to ignite the half-lamppost – though the term was used less to describe a landmark than to designate a broad geographical area. It was not far from the post itself, however, that I spotted on my way up the road from my house that evening the scoffable brown cords of a stumpy individual and the odious camouflage jacket of an unacceptably lanky one.

'Hiya.'

'Hiya.'

'Well?'

'Well?' Vomit leaned back against the sad post. A low sky flowed over our heads.

'Will we do it?'

'Dunno.'

I yawned and let them talk.

It constantly surprised me, it surprised me once again as I looked about, that our area lacked true girls. True girls only lived somewhere else, elusively. A woman was watching us while chamoising her window.

'We get the number of the UDA off Beamer, right?' Vomit was explaining. A car screeched past.

'Is Beamer a Prod or something?'

My question inspired a less than dignified expectoration from Vomit roughly equivalent in language to: Wise up! At our school? They continued to go over the details, but I was preoccupied by lower things. I stared dreamily back at the woman, trying to unzip her dress without her feeling it and peel off the strappy contraption of a bra. She jiggled her breasts for me as she waved her chamois. To me it seemed preposterous and wonderful that she would want her windows to be pristine while the façade of her house was almost graffitied over with IRA and GET OUT.

'Ring up on Saturday morning, right?' Vomit was verifying. 'Say Turner's recruiting for the Ra.'

'Do you want to?'

'I don't care.'

I sat up on a low wall and smiled provocatively at a soldier leading a foot patrol. The woman blatantly tried to peer up and down the road with an anxious frown, reinforcing her identity as a snob. The graffiti on her house came undoubtedly in response to the fact that it was painted an ostentatious blue.

'Write it on a piece of paper. One of us'll read it out.'

'In a different accent.'

'Good thinking, Brains.'

'Will we?'

'Suppose so.'

A Pepsi bottle smashed beside Vomit's foot. 'What else is there to do?' he said. It looked as though a riot was imminent. We decided to shift.

'We'll go to our house,' said Bleep. He proposed, having come across seasickness tablets in the medicine cabinet in his house and having noted that they contained codeine, that we now try to get high in celebration of our brand new concept. So we scuffed up the hill to his house and bald bedroom to plan further and eat Quells. There followed a bleak evening of, 'I think I can feel something,' 'Can you?' 'Maybe not,' and much time devoted to worrying about the perils of overdosing on four tablets. Bleep tried to retch in a panic at the last minute and failed, while I, supine on the bed, awaited a visit by sensation. It was a patient and sober wait ending in self-contempt, with rain at the window, Bleep's mother shouting downstairs, Bleep's ashamed eyes, doors banging and agreement that Vomit and I had overstayed our welcome. My image of us as fated to the glamour of vice and abandon was proving difficult to sustain. But we were, I can affirm as I reflect on it, anything that evening but *compos mentis*.

We fixed a time and a place to meet to begin the execution of our plot: ten o'clock, Saturday, my house.

Using a domestic phone for our purposes was out of the question. Our area was a magnificent telecommunications theme park of tracing, tapping, bugging, snoopiness on party lines, interfering with poles, do-it-yourself extensions that put kitchen gossip on army radios. So we had to set out on the dreaded day from my front door with our secret number and our scrawled message, at nearer to noon than ten, for the closest kiosk. My estate had, at the bottom of the street, a bombed-out shell – implausible container of human excrement and contraceptives, its royal red slopped over with the obligatory green (for Eire) and concluded with a paint bomb (to grey). Heading out of the estate, we walked together up the street towards the main road. An amplified voice scratched the air unintelligibly.

'Right, where is there one?' Vomit said as we came into the heavy traffic. We scanned the road. The clouds were splashed with muddy water. Bleep and I glanced at each other uneasily. Vomit dug into his hair. Across the road a man was bawling at a microphone.

'But,' Bleep offered unsurely, 'aren't they all smashed?'

I perched on a random metal pole and smirked. Bleep's eyes darted, promising a blush. But Vomit glowered with the effort to keep his countenance. Vomit was entirely bent on holding all together as chaos threatened. It was Vomit who kept us at that moment, though only by an eyebrow, from spinning off back into the void, the domain of sleepwalkers and all the aimless ones from which we had only just emerged triumphant and hooting with a purpose. Vomit would not let the admission be made that if we had been relying on finding a telephone in our area *in working order* then all our preparations, what we were glad to think of as our master tactics, were truly no better than, no different from, any odious schoolboy sniggerings over an ink pellet! And even though bilious pillar boxes had their scalps ripped off, zebra crossings were skinned of their stripes, elongated DEAD SLOW markings rendered YOU'RE DEAD, traffic lights swiped, Belisha beacons pocketed and even the very footpaths in places rendered inoperative, Vomit, by that hot frown and peeling impatience, was forbidding us outright to betray any doubt in our search for order. 'I can't see one near,' he faked.

Some people were delaying near the man with the microphone. He was shouting at them, 'What's wrong with youse!' Bleep watched uneasily. I had no political conscience and, provided I could keep my kneecaps, I had only sneers for our revolutionary brothers, so I felt no pang of guilt in recognizing now that our aim for services as normal reversed all expectation of us. Still, it was wise to get off the scene. I peered gingerly down the road in the direction of the cemetery.

'Down there,' I suggested. Some of the passing cars sounded their horns in support of the man. 'What about down there?' We stared for a moment. I was hoping, though I felt it best not to mention, that we might come upon females in this direction naturally straying in their kinky uniforms, even though today was Saturday.

'Right,' said Bleep eagerly.

Vomit let out a worried 'Mmm' and said, 'It's rough.'

'Not really,' I said. 'We'd get a kiosk down there.'

'There's a chance,' said Bleep. Vomit nodded, so with some faith that down there a solution lay, we set off towards the cemetery.

It began to brighten. Vomit did most of the talking in isolated sentences, invariably along the lines of: This'll teach him a lesson. As we skirted the cemetery clouds lodged between the chimneys of an old factory. The traffic was pulling out round a burning car. 'This is mad,' he continued to mumble. He was nervous. There were white handkerchiefs drooping from most of the lampposts. In spite of my ignorance of these things — impressive enough to inspire pride — I could not pretend to be unaware that these had been strung up the summer before during more hungerstriking and that, though the rain had now washed the dye out of them, they had been meant to serve as tiny mourning flags. Clearly, I concluded, we were still safe in a Catholic area. I decided that this detail of the handkerchiefs was, to cynics like Bleep and me, probably worth a grunt of recognition, so I sighed, 'Ah, look,' nudging him: 'We surrender.' He shrugged his shoulders — from him a strong sign of approval.

'This is useless,' Vomit sighed. There were no kiosks about. But Bleep spoke over his words.

'Is that a phone?'

We squinted. It was difficult to say if it was or not without the lively, eyecatching, vital red to go by. A greyish, greenish daub on the far footpath did almost resemble in shape at least one side of a kiosk. And, in effect, that is what it proved to be: a solitary door to nowhere, standing clean in a concrete base, one part green, nine parts grey. I gave an exasperated smack through my lips.

'Let's get off this crappy road,' Bleep said, so at the next turning on the right we diverted our course down a dilapidated treelined hill. The light was clotting.

'Go over the plan again,' Vomit said, being mature. I felt a tear of rain.

'I ring up,' Bleep sighed with a dubious glance at me.

'Remember the accent.'

'And what do you say?'

'I've it written down, haven't I!'

'What do you say anyway?'

'Remember the accent.'

We broke into a kids' game of football. Somewhere a fire was burning. I ran an eye over the side streets as Bleep went through his exhausted performance of booming into a mimed telephone with any authority he could muster — Greg Turner of whatever street he lived on was regularly coercing kids to join the IRA . . . he, a leading citizen who shall remain nameless, was just about sick of it . . . his whole loyalist community expected that Turner character to be no less than shot for it . . . Soon my attention was everywhere else: between dustbins, in the hedges, up the driveways, through gardens of rubble, panning round at a pitch of readiness hoping to identify — by that unmistakable reddish tinge that had so pleased my black-and-white eyes — girls! But by the time we had come up to a busy roundabout the only femininity I had seen was a naked doll being chewed by a dog, a boy who resembled a girl from behind and who shrieked, 'What're you smilin' at!' and an obese lonely woman leaning on her garden gate cursing everything, including the very air: 'Look at that fuckin' air!' A man's voice called after us, 'Whata youse want?' and then, 'Hey, Cream Socks!' Vomit glanced bashfully at his socks. If we could think of our wanderings as a miniature *Aeneid*, this was surely a visit to the Underworld. Separately, we dashed through the traffic to the far footpath. At last Bleep made it across on his stunted legs, and we resumed.

'And then you hang up.'

'Mm.'

'Okay.'

'Do you think he'll get shot?'

'Hope so.'

'Kneecapped anyway.'

I tutted. 'Jammy bastard.'

We joined another road off the roundabout. Up ahead there

were some soldiers standing about laughing. Together they formed a shrub of camouflage that broke the monotony of paving. Vomit dropped his voice: 'Where're we going?'

Yet before he could get an answer, and rather more swiftly than can be recounted, we were spreadeagled against one side of a jeep. Normally this was a trivial enough routine provided you were polite; but Bleep started up too polite.

'Empty your pockets,' a mustachioed soldier silenced him. Everything went on to the bonnet of the jeep: nibbled biro top, locker keys, ball of fluff and that slip of paper from which Bleep was going to read.

My legs started to wobble. If they read that, my mind was racing, it could be real-life internment maybe! The soldier stroked the things, and as a subordinate frisked us I kept my eyes on the note, folded in a half-open, twitching, inviting V. It was begging to be explored, irresistible, I thought, it was obvious he would read it. Any normal redblooded fingers would be itching to undo it and smooth it out pale and prostrate . . .

'Turn round,' he shouted suddenly. 'What's this?' His accent pierced the smoke.

It was then, all at once, as I quivered under this godlike authority, that I recognized my naked self. Until then I had only been passing by in a cloud of vagueness. This voice instantly dispersed it and what remained were bare facts. That slip of paper was proof of a murder plot, it was as good as a plea of guilty to malice aforethought. Before it had seemed natural to ignore mere details like these. But not any longer. Now for the first time I was goggling at the unsightly truth. There would be no dozing on the fat border between yes and no beneath these fact fanatics. Their certainty had muscles which bruised the air. With them there was no neutral zone reserved for childish fickleness . . .

'What's this?' he repeated.

I sickened. I saw my meek parents suddenly involved and me puling with feigned astonishment, 'It was a joke.' How had this all happened in a moment, I puzzled: here was the army of Great Britain being literal about a blur and a daydream. I was about to pipe up, 'That's his note,' and point to Duffy. Vomit would verify it. But the soldier spoke again.

'They're car keys.' He was holding up our locker keys.

'They're my locker keys,' Vomit was saying. My heart was boxing on the wall of my chest. 'They're locker keys.'

'Where d'you live?'

'Well, we actually live in, you see . . .' That note was shifting in the breeze.

'What you doing round here? Doing cars, right?'

'They're locker keys.' Vomit gesticulated like a reasonable revolutionary. 'We've lockers in school. They're locker keys.'

The soldier jabbed his finger forward. 'I'll put you inside that fucking jeep in a minute.' Vomit dropped his hands. Behind another soldier was singing our addresses into a radio. 'You shouldn't be out of your area.'

Bleep volunteered: 'We're going for a walk.' The radio crackled. The soldier wrung his face in disbelief.

'A *walk!*' We looked at each other with innocent surprise. He frowned. 'Take your things.' We clutched everything. 'Don't go out of your area in future,' he bawled as we sidled off. We felt their camouflage on the backs of our necks.

The road was leading up into the city centre. Whatever bitterness Bleep and Vomit were thinking, my regrets were possibly quite particular. Now that the cloud around me had been blasted away, everything was clear: I was not remotely concerned to find a telephone kiosk. Indeed, it said everything about the boylike primates I hung around with that they had allowed me to coax them into the epicentre of Catholic deprivation, the heart of the ghetto, in search of a functioning telephone – unless they too had each been privately seeking the same as myself – or something else? My regret was that no bevy of girls had run up to us with moist comforts. I had been in search of gentleness. As we came into the centre we were in no mood for talking. We saw a vinegary hamburger joint. Vomit licked his lips.

'What did they want to know all that for anyway?' said Vomit when we were sitting round a table.

'That's a good question, dickhead,' I said. Neither he nor Bleep were as stung as I was by the episode. Perhaps we were in no position to be righteous, I thought to myself, but, all the same, no one should tell us that we had to keep to our area. There was nothing there except Quells and cough bottles on Saturday evenings. The both of them munched away. I simply sat staring out at a policeman waving traffic on with his machine gun. There were no shoppers on the street. It was turning to evening, peaceful apart from, somewhere, the clicking of a metal turnstile.

Eventually Bleep said, 'What'll we do?'

Vomit was scratching his flaky arm over the table. I looked out of the window again instead of answering. A newspaper blew against the policeman. 'This is good, isn't it,' I said at last. Bleep looked straight at me with his long stupid eyelashes.

'Yeah,' he said.

'What is?'

He knitted his brows, trying to find a witticism, and at last settled on: 'Yeah.'

Exasperated, I stood up and the three of us straggled out into the dirty pallor. It had got windy. We walked round to queue for a black taxi into our area. A dog was pissing against a telephone kiosk. We stopped.

'That's a phone,' I said.

'So what?'

'What do you mean, "So what?"' Vomit laughed.

'That's a false laugh,' said Bleep.

'You're a false person.'

I opened the door with my weight and lifted the receiver. 'It's working,' I said.

'Well?'

'Well?' said Bleep.

It was beginning to rain. I tried to be amusing. 'Duffius,' I croaked, 'the answer — utmost speed.' Birds were watching us from a wire.

'*This* isn't logical, anyway.' He tried a superior sigh.

Vomit shook his head and said, with all the Apollonian dryness he could concentrate, 'What's the point.' The breeze was blowing him to flakes. But something was reassuring me at this moment, it was perhaps our destiny. Here, after all, was what we were supposed to be looking for, a genuine working telephone, unignorably, indeed proudly, royally red.

'We might as well,' I suggested. I wedged myself in the door.

'What do you think?' Vomit asked. Bleep thought for a moment. A tin thrashed past his foot.

'It's murder,' he answered.

'So fuck!' I said loudly.

He looked at Vomit. 'I don't mind,' he said.

'We might as well,' said Vomit.

We all got into the kiosk. Bleep ferreted for the slip of paper. A piece of one of the windows was lying on the shelf inside like a big set square. 'What's the number?'

We sniggered. I dialled it as Bleep pressed the receiver hard against his ear. We all heard the ringing tone. It kept ringing. Suddenly he slammed his hand on the rest. He burst out laughing. 'I'm not ready.' Vomit's face was wooden. I started to redial. 'No, I want to rehearse.' I squeezed round and squinted out through the smoky plastic while Bleep attempted a convincing adult voice. 'Greg Turner of twenty-seven . . .' he hummed. A police jeep crawled past the semi-detacheds. '. . . and we want him wiped out for good!'

'Look,' I said, 'perfect, we haven't got all day.' I angled the slip of paper in his hand towards me and dialled the number again.

'Jesus!' He crossed his legs. We heard the ringing tone again. It rang and rang. And then, strangely, Bleep turned away from us. The drone faltered. He put a finger in his ear, frowning. Vomit smiled. The slip of paper was trembling. His voice was loud. I looked away with a grin. Suddenly, he wrenched an arm up through the squash of our bodies and, with a karate chop, cut himself off. He looked at us, breathless, expectant. We looked back at him so he said, 'It was a woman answered.' After a minute Vomit mumbled, 'We've actually done it.'

'I know,' I said.

'We shouldn't have.' We looked at each other. 'It was really banal.'

'I know,' said Bleep.

On the way round to the black taxis and in the queue we said nothing. It was raining invisibly. When our turn came we squeezed in with three women who nattered all the way up the road. Until we got out of the taxi to part at the corner we had exchanged no words since the kiosk. 'See you,' I said, breaking the silence.

'See you.'

We made off in different directions. Well, I admitted to myself on the walk to my street, it was a selfish thing to do. The whole long day lay behind us in a disgraceful trail. Some skinheads were lolling against our wall. For me, at any rate, the adventure had been barren; though, at the same time there was an assurance that at last we had acted. We had done something which was better than our grey, brooding, morose wait to be older before we would start to live. I walked stiffly past the skinheads. Today we had made a choice, it was clear, stark. Perhaps for the first time, I thought, we were really ourselves, distinctly unwise and ungentle — that was how I saw it. I would stew in selfishness and banality and badness and anything else before I would let a scruple stop me from kicking out this time. At anything. Yes, I could see it now in its true colours. That unloved skimpy man at the front of our class had never spared a blind wank for our pains and fears. Now, I said to myself as I glided through the little gate to my house, now it was we who were laughing. There would be no heroics, no wailing and lamentation of women at his last pretty hour. So what if we punctured the fatuous hot air out of his one clapped-out lung? I could see him wheeze as the gunshot reverberated, a trickle of blood down his quivering chin, his spindle legs would buckle and he would be down, red eyes blinking for mercy. Beautiful!

IV

STREET MAGIC

———————————

BUT TOMAS WAS never in the humour for convincing Paula so she just heard over and over, 'It's a long story.' He told her no more than that he was waiting for a thing that was soon to come, a mindblowing thing. He spoke of this with borrowed eyes that fixed a distant judgment in the grubby sunlight. Then he'd sort of twinkle and take her hand and press it and, say they were on their way to a bar, it was like they owned the road the way they drifted over shadows of fugacious clouds. She wouldn't quiz him on his big break. She knew enough — what business he was doing. One day months before she'd seen him walk to the quay. She'd hung back and watched as he stood outside the jakes. His face, when she caught sight of it in the day's sticky dazzle, had a bare simplicity. It seemed delighted to splash for hours in the dirty shade rippling at the entrance. She wasn't disgusted: it had burned her up with desire.

Inside her she thought: Shit, what a difference in him! They'd been waiting for the spring to be happy in Dublin, but when they'd first arrived it had freaked him out. For months he'd walked around on his own and sat moodily and she'd promised herself they'd give it till the summer. Now that it was May, a great rotting ball in the sky, he was himself again, making eyes, carefree. 'We're gonna be reekin' with money soon,' he gladdened her. 'This crap's only a bad spell. Right?'

He was there some days by one to catch any lunchtime

business and the trickle of scumbags just out of bed. Or sometimes she'd glimpse him later when the action must have slowed to a pause, waiting, chatting on the quay to another randy angel, leaning over the wall, maybe spinning rays of spit to the river. This wasn't his scene, it was a brief mad buzz he and she were on together. As for the surprise outcome, she would go along with that, she thought, for a bit. Because it wasn't like it was too much hopefulness that had dashed them to the capital from their town further north with its hankerings amid chimney smoke and winds of manure, its concrete glazed with dreamlife: it was too much need for it.

Paula had protection from disasters, she'd seen it again and again. So she felt safe enough, and she felt he was just too shy to do anything heavy. Anyway, she trusted him. He'd even told her what he was doing was dodgy, just hadn't filled her in. He wouldn't tell a cruel lie. It was his good nature she'd fallen for, more manly than the malice and jittery sinews of Fran, a guy back home whose lack she saw more clearly than ever when Tomas came out with things like: 'It's all your fate, you can't change it, believe me Paula.' Her former guy was an acidhead. And he was that lapsed cliché, couldn't permit faith in anything because faith sounded Catholic. And besides, while he'd blown her welfare on tripledips and cans and kebabs, now in Dublin Tomas was coming back with scores and tenners scrunched up into beads. When she took them she pictured those scumbags' yellow thighs, but she was down-to-earth about it. She thought, and she was on the point of teasing him in the bath once as she kissed a patch of grime: 'Where there's muck there's money. Right?'

And their unhappiness was okay. They went to nite clubs. They sat in chippers like they were waiting to make new friends. Then one day Tomas brought in one of the guys from the flat below theirs. They discussed in front of her, just messing. Men were individual but women weren't that evolved. She gave out: 'D'you believe that, you?' She tutted. 'No.' He straightened his face. 'I like girls.'

He was called Fish. He wore tracksuit bottoms with pin holes burnt in them and pointy slip-ons and had snarled hair. Soon they all started sitting up late in his flat drinking and talking over videos. Fish had lots to say about his life while his cousin Sammy had no personality, he was an unphysical boy, half made of light, it seemed to Paula, maybe constantly conversing in an invisible style with the dead. Fish talked intensively about 'great friends' and people with 'dead-on personalities' in a way that excluded his cousin and involved Tomas and Paula. She sat with her finger in his fist. Scratching his miraculous Medal, Fish entertained, recollected the first time he plucked a crab off him when he was fifteen – he was so outraged he'd kept it lusting in an upturned glass. Paula just listened. He produced hash. And with him it was no paranoid buzz, now they got on top of hash. He told them what bars to hate, what clubs to obsess. He was into reggae. They mellowed out and giggled a bit. He asked Paula did she know who to borrow from. She said no. He started rolling another and said did she want to hear a story about how his granny had got that wrong and lost her fingers. She had come here from America, a really nice woman. Paula was happy to get all this suss. She said, 'yeah,' and made Tomas listen. Fish was good at talking.

He explained how when his granny died a gang walked right into the funeral parlour and cut her fingers off to get the rings. 'But she was only in a coma, right, Paula?' He flicked the spliff with his nail and bit off the twist. 'She opened her eyes. The gang nearly died of fright. Dropped her fingers and legged it. Can you see it, Paula?' He held the spliff ready to light while he finished describing how she'd climbed out of the coffin and wandered home a bit dazed. 'Me old one had a heart attack when she saw her.'

'I don't believe that,' laughed Paula.

'It's true.'

'How is she now?' Tomas asked.

'Grand,' he said. 'She sells up town.'

As time went on Tomas's tongue loosened too. Once or twice when they were walking through town he came out with stuff she'd never heard before in her life, weird stuff about pentacles and wands and meditating and planets. 'Stop,' she said with a laugh, using one of Fish's words. Yet there were other moments when Tomas's certainty was infectious. Like every time she kept him going about a proper job and that gaze would train on something behind the glare. It was like he could picture a sparkling horizon lapping at the backs of the high moth-eaten, dove-possessed buildings on the quay. Or a moist dawn about to break on the dull red streets behind that were always full of fumes and warm shade and where odd cars cruised in the early afternoon.

As they waited she got hooked on their life, on all the stupid things: like waking on stains, sometimes late, to distant lorries rumbling and a bluish-grey haze that stuck to things in the room. She was hooked on the way they played as they dressed, on the feel of his bare foot on her cunt, even on nipping out for white bread and milk to the shop on the corner among fresh dust and birdsong. They'd have evening breakfasts. Then when he threw his jacket on she'd maybe delay him by giving his tongue a suck. 'What're you doin', Paula?' 'Kissin' you, you prick.' When he went she'd spend her time on the big streets going into cafés, asking for a job. She'd hold her head up as she walked and breathe in buses and warmth and crowds and splinters of sun. Kids sat about begging in rags. Sometimes she ran into friends of Fish: Snakey and Donna with people whose names she never knew. 'What's the story, Paula?' the slimey smackhead would say and she'd go to bars with them and join in some of their chat.

'Where's Tomas?' She'd tell them what he'd told her to say: 'He's makin' good moves, stockin', drivin' cars.' They liked you to talk yourself up.

One late afternoon she walked from them through rising heat and a smell of tarmac to a bar to meet him. There was a fat beat from a top window. She hated her own sweat as she waited inside the bar. He turned up smiling. 'How's the business?' she began. He said it was cool. Then she thought she'd ask him about that opportunity. He shrugged.

'It was bullshit,' he said.

'You said you were certain,' she reminded him softly.

'I was wrong then.'

They drank and leaned against each other and he reassured her this was just a run of bad luck. Then they reeled home to bed while it was still light.

She brought up the subject of the bullshit again one night in bed.

'Forget it,' he yawned.

'Tell us.'

So he told her the whole story, disjointed, mumbling. Told her how in early May he'd met a guy. They'd got talking, he'd sussed that Tomas needed money. He'd called himself a Druid. 'He was a mad bloke,' Tomas told her, 'into all mad things.' For a minute he didn't say any more and Paula realized she was gripping his cock with her gentle fist. She slapped his thigh.

'Go on.'

'He was a mad bastard,' Tomas tutted. 'He said he could get me loads of money and all. I asked how.'

'How?'

He sighed, mumbled, 'He did a spell or somethin'.'

'Did he?'

He rolled on his side away from her. 'So now you know.'

She whispered, 'What did you have to do?' He didn't speak.

She tried to coax him. His cock was curled up asleep now. He wouldn't say more.

She lay and wondered. If there was one thing that should be true, it seemed to her, it was a spell, because there was no way to change your life without one. She remembered how when she was younger she'd kept seeing a boy when their parents had all been against it. She'd said to him, 'We can make it happen, Dessie, with the power of thought,' and nodded to him with confidence and her ponytail tapped her from behind. The more she'd persisted the more unlikely obstacles popped up. After that she'd stopped trying to make things happen at all, she'd started waiting for whatever was meant to come. Nothing ever came. Her mother had told her, 'You can never beat life,' and she'd realized that was dead right. 'But you have to keep tryin'.' Before she and Tomas had left with excited reluctance for Dublin she'd tried once again to get her act together. She'd applied for courses, she'd tried to get work as a waitress in every farflung and scabby snack bar and canteen, she'd applied for jobs for Tomas. It was like pushing a wall. As she looked at him sleeping now she thought: We were born poor, we're fated to live among shit. To want to change your fate was right. It was well right. And she burrowed her fingers through his and lay and heard him mutter once, twice.

After that they both felt down for a bit and didn't talk much. Tomas and Fish spent a lot of time together. A flavour of crap was getting in the flat from the street like the brightness gone bad. She started wearing her hair up. Then one evening Tomas broke some news. 'I have a job!'

'What?'

'Come on, we're goin' out.' And they went to a bar. Paula asked more. He just said a guy was getting him a job soon.

'What guy?' she asked.

'A guy, right?'

'Where did you meet him?'

'It's a hundred per cent fact, Paula.'

'What job is it?'

'Don't believe me then, I don't care.'

So she didn't ask more. But a few weeks later when she was in town one day she had another squint across the river. The buildings were shimmering and fawn. Dazzle moved on the quay like spirits, maybe disappointed to find out what their relatives were at. She could make him out talking to tough-looking guys with cropped hair while boy scouts went in and out. As she stood now she wasn't imagining his various filthy blisses, she was thinking about the million lives going on along-side his which she never saw, the ordinary lives of young guys on the road with moustaches or shoulder bags, lives folding around them as they walked away. More subtle lives. More real. Guys nodded at other guys and she wondered what they knew. Then she wondered: Could it be that they seemed happy only because they hid the crap in their lives and didn't fight it like her and Tomas?

A nervous tramp came up to her and asked her directions. She shook her head, walked away. She pushed herself through the almost tropical summer and made herself feel good by pretending Dublin was a much more interesting place, an unknowable city. She ran into Fish on a big road lined with dusty palms. He wore a baby's shades. 'You're one of our own, Paula' he said, 'Let's get *there*, let's get *home* . . . to a bar.' He blessed himself passing a church.

Fish, it turned out, wasn't all Irish, and she sat imagining somewhere in Egypt. She asked where he got money. He settled more into his seat. He said he lived off a claim he'd got when he was eighteen for fifty-six thousand: when he was a kid some cleric, handy with cuffs on the ear, had administered a freak one, concussed him. Paula didn't drink much. Soon they walked to a hotel bar. 'Take my hand, right?' he said. 'For luck.' There she had coffee and he drank more. Later when they stepped out on to the street he tried to coax her to go somewhere else, she said she couldn't but walked a little way with him. She held his sinewy arm. 'You'd suit your hair short,' he said. They parted. She strayed back to the flat past kids burning a tyre and went to bed. She sweated too much to sleep.

Later Tomas came in, a bit spaced. She rolled over with her arse sticking up so he would pat it. He talked in bed thinking he should cheer her up. He told her a story. When he was younger and at home, he giggled, he'd been sitting on his bed wanking with his eyes closed and a Walkman on. He giggled a bit more and then carried on. When he'd opened his eyes there was a mug of tea on the bedside table. 'My old one,' he said, cracking up laughing.

She didn't react. She'd never known him so talkative, it wasn't like him. The early morning traffic had begun, aeroplanes on their way to places. 'Why should that guy give you a job?' she said.

'D'you not believe in friendship, fuck it!' He rolled over. She threw another blanket off them. She decided: I'll give it till September.

And she saw Fish in bars in the afternoons. There was nothing to do but talk and pant and drink. Europe was on tongues: how could Danish porn ever defeat the spinster virgins who marched around town jerking posters — 'Porn Causes Rape' stencilled on the sides of cardboard boxes. She asked Fish was Tomas going on about anything these days. He thought and answered vaguely how he'd told him they should be positive and make things go their way or something. She knew there was something there that Fish had never thought about. He wasn't into it, he was already talking, telling her about his cousin. Sammy was actually one in a million or one in ten thousand or something. Froth put a little moustache on Fish. At one time, he confided, he'd been thinking that his cousin might have been queer. And there was a point when his cousin started thinking this too, but he wasn't sure. Fish paused. He picked his teeth. She loosened her sleeves. He went on. He told her that he'd come to the conclusion at last that his cousin was asexual. He asked her with a laugh had she ever heard of that. 'Not really,' she said. On his own his cousin had actually found out that this was the case from a doctor. Fish began to snigger. 'And he thought this was really like a tragedy, right? D'you know what I'm saying, Paula?' Sweat rolled on his cheek like hysterical laughs. 'But at least he knew!'

'Is he really that?' Paula asked.

'What?'

'Is he what you said?'

'One in a million,' said Fish.

At last it rained. One morning in September when Paula and Tomas woke up the garden was drenched. She recognized the smack of wet phlox. They had tea and caramel eggs and she said lightly, 'When are you gettin' that job, Tomas?'

'It fell through, the bastard,' he said.

She nodded and smiled. 'You're a bastard,' she told him, and the rain started pouring inside her eyes as well. 'You're full of shit.'

Now she didn't know what to do. She went out and got a bus into town. I'm spiralling down, she thought. A woman passed her in the street, crying. To give herself a purpose she went and got her hair cut. She wanted to pray, she believed in praying, praying would be playing her last card – but it spooked her, God was so negative. He would only give relief from pain, never anything positive. A few times in the past she'd begged for something she wanted from a guardian angel she pictured behind the air. The result had always been dramatic, but the answer was cruel. Very rapidly she'd got what she'd asked for, but with something mischievous tagged on. She remembered the clearest example and she related it to Fish that evening when they met. For many years while she was at school, she explained to him in the corner of a crowded snug, she never had a boyfriend. 'It's true, Fish, I was really depressed.' One night she was specially low because she had to turn up at a party on her own. On her way through the garden to the flat where the party was she was psyching herself up and she made, she explained, this great intense plea that she would meet someone there. Fish bobbed his head. One of her mates was at that party, she'd been thinking about trying to fix Paula up. She introduced this boy to her. He had freckles and ginger hair. They got talking. 'I think Paula's a lovely name,' he'd said. 'My sister has a friend called Paula, she's dead quiet, so she is.' He was better than nothing, she'd thought, at least he had a mouth she could kiss, a body she could touch. Fish bounced closer. At one point in the party, she went on, he took his hand out of his pocket to secure a crisp bag on his lap while he picked from it. The hand was deformed. His fingers were like crushed toes. With corns. The first thing she'd thought was: It's a message that I shouldn't be so selfish and want a body.

Fish shook his head, 'Oh don't say that, Paula, that's stupid.' And he started stroking her hair. She went along with it.

She didn't any more, she told him. Now she didn't have a clue, she just wondered if it was simply meant to stop her getting her way. 'You know if you're a bastard,' she said, 'it all falls in your lap. But you see if you're sensitive . . .'

Fish was stroking her hand. Maybe this time Tomas was right to believe you could have your way if you were positive. Fish slid his arm around her. 'D'you understand it, Fish?' she said. 'Life?' Suddenly he put his lips on her cheek. She waited, smelling his Guinness.

When she turned to face him he was examining her mouth. She kept thinking as his hand went up her blouse. She couldn't deny what she thought. It seemed to her life would always go against her needs. Cruelly and deliberately. And she knew that if there was a God he would have a long maroon tongue, toad legs, bat wings. She didn't tell Fish how it ended with that boy with a hand like a foot. She'd actually gone out with him. It was the rumour that his arse was freckled that decided her to blank him. Now Fish was scratching her back.

'I hate me,' she muttered. 'I do . . . being me . . .'

'You're not,' he said into her neck.

They walked back to the house together with their arms looped and she wondered was his hand on his hip. When Tomas saw her he looked at her hair. 'Where were you Paula?'

'Job huntin', right?'

He shrugged.

But a week later, without mentioning, she moved out. She finally decided Tomas was no good. A poxy but cheap bedsit had come up. She was going to get a job in Dublin or she was going to go back home. But either one of these seemed like the wrong move. One morning Fish called out there. They ate Toffee Crisps as they waited for the bells of a cathedral to stop. She hated those mangled bells like the voice of a devil. When there was quiet he told her that Tomas had left the flat and moved in with some bloke. She sat down sneering. He looked at his wrapper. And now he sort of almost proposed to her, he asked her would she move in with him. She stood up. She paced up and down. 'Would you?' he said. He took her hand, tweaking her fingers.

'What about your cousin?' she asked.

'He's dead,' he said. 'Did you not hear? He was in a crash, there was metal touchin' his brain. Oh, it was terrible They had to cut him out of the car and all, so they did . . .'

'Is that true?'

'Yeah.' He folded his arms. She stared at him. 'What?' He laughed like she was picking on him.

She took herself for an evening roam somewhere she'd never

been, around high towers of corporation flats, deliquescent, sensing Heaven. Every face seemed ugly, with too much detail, cheeks were too big. She wasn't imagining some other city now, because she couldn't think of anywhere more unknowable. Dublin had gone bogey on her, the thing to do was leave. A fat leaf fell on a burnt-out car. Yeah, I'll move in, she thought.

From then on she tried to forget about Tomas, and every time she was in town she made sure she didn't look across the wet distance at the quay. But one day on her way to meet Fish she ran into him again. Now he had cropped hair that didn't suit his clothes, made him look violent. His jacket was an elegant shade of grey that matched the sky. 'What's the story?' she said, a bit blown out by the gear. He looked like he was well into it these days, getting big money, reeking with it. 'Have you cracked life?'

'Well, I know what I think,' he said moodily. 'I know now everyone just fuckin' uses everyone, right?'

'Yeah?'

'Life's evil, Paula, that's my opinion. You have to be evil for this world.'

'Are you right this time?'

'It's a hundred per cent fact, Paula. Believe me, you have to be clued in.'

As they walked their separate ways she didn't let herself get upset, she told herself that Tomas was in the past, a better time was coming. She joined Fish and laughed as they walked across the river to a bar. Everywhere there were salty bus fumes and pigeon shit and empurpled passers-by. Fish knew something was up so he gossiped, talked about anything to keep her glowing. 'You just don't believe in anything,' she kidded him as they drank. Soon she relaxed and she decided to tell him the whole story of Tomas's spell. She took her time over telling it, embroidering most of it and buzzing off him as they drank.

V

———————

HARVESTMAN

———————————

TAKE BEINGS. Beings need happiness. True? Take me. I am a being. I want salt. I want air. I want happiness. These are essentials for each and every day. Picture life without them. Life would be not as it should.

Take me dumping my scraps. The bin in my cooking section gets full, so full no more scraps fit in. This is natural. This is pile-up. Things pile up, things spill out. I am just explaining the essentials. Dump the bad is an essential. Healthy and clean. I am in my cooking section.

You can share in today's thought. First I will depict my surroundings. Close your eyelids. Try to see it. Evening. I wash up. Sticky smell — to my shame. Lorries ramming along on the motorway below. Belt of sky. Me. Pool of light in the flat flavour of perfume which I compare to a young lady's perfume. I call this 'atmosphere'. I stand thinking on my feet. I stand by the big pane. I am washing up by the sink. The spoon is a utensil. For a utensil the spoon is one of the things for which I have a lot of time. I shall say something by the by. Spoons are relative. Spoonful of love. Take your time and enjoy that saw. I rub the spoon. I stand liking it. Consider this: together we can all appreciate the feminine touch, Black man, White man. Below are voices. I look down from the window.

Sometimes I do get a very filled-up head. I stand and think. One of the things I think is as follows: this room is a disgrace. I get filled up with being furious at me. I am looking at the kitchen bin. It is overdue to dump. I am getting my jacket. I am just doing what has to be done. Start and finish. I am not getting into extremes. We need balance. I look for shoes. I find them. Getting into shoes is all I am doing. Going down to dump my kitchen's bin is the extent of it. People say, 'Moderation in all things.' The simple bare necessities. I sit with my shoes. My neck is hot. I unbutton my collar. I listen and soak in the atmosphere. Not much noise is now happening out there. I inspect the air. That is rain coming. That is called 'murk'. That is distinct blue 'murk'. Pessimistic. I am thinking for a bit. That is a long way down. I sit whilst thinking. Traffic brushes by. By the by, that traffic is a vulgarity. The traffic is vinegar on chips. Those stairs can take it out of you. Definite. They can take it out of me. Do you understand? I take off my jacket. I will dump later. I replace my shoes. Tell me this. Do you understand? I just want to get on with tidying, that is all. Put a face on the place. I wipe my pipes. Rebrillo the tap. What more is there to say? I do those things and I do my necessaries.

One hour later I am in my cooking section. I will be open with you. The feeling is mutual. I am talking about share. Share and share alike. I shall tell you about what is happening. I have dished out blancmange now being in process of swallowing it. Not so much enjoying it as so-so. Blancmange is a question of economics. Milton Keynes. Inevitably I smell the tin cans. I smell old vegetables. This is rubbish. Scraps. I look at my bin supposing I should dump it. How can I have clean surrounds with a smell? That is what I am thinking when all of a sudden what is on the lino? Guess. Share today's thought. I will tell you. What is beside my bin's rim in a tea spill on the lino? My last blancmange is in the dish. Guess. I shall tell you. A being. I can describe it. A ball. From that ball go five-and-a-half legs to different directions. I did count them whilst eating. He cannot move. Long poky legs like spokes which are damaged. It no longer is the true shape of a windmilliform invertebrate. You can use the term 'windmilliform'. Use your Collins. Do you know the name for this 'asteriskous' creature? You can use the term 'asteriskous'. I happen to know the name of this creature. But I need not say it. I know the word. And so? Why boast? It has no importance. I feel like eating. I sneak a glance at my remaining blancmange. I think the following. Please follow this. He is having it rough. Please do not stand on top of him. I think it is humiliating to be such a fellow trying to hobble out of a tea spill under a rotten bin on bits of snipped legs. Can you follow? I am trying to put it across to you. A being needs legs. A home. Flies. Independence. Try to follow this. A being needs a lifestyle, a partner. Love. I am explaining so you can consider. Is that fair or is that not fair? I hear your thoughts. You would call him a no-big-deal being. Wrong. Let yourself be corrected, sir. Do not stand on him. What use would a bit of bitty spokes and juice be? Do not judge. God's creatures creep and God's creatures crawl. Egalitarian. Give him a break. A good time is coming. That is not just juicy waste for the dump. That might be thinking of Heaven. Thus, is no dead soul. That is a 'harvestman'. Which happens to be the name which you now know. I am going to clean up the flat. But I am not going to squash him. He can live for a better day. The vicissitudes of life. First I eat. My flat is all over the shop. Stack of rubbish on the floor. Creatures. Your home is your castle. Agree? A lady is shouting outside. I stop thinking.

I ask myself where I was. Blancmange perfection. My bin is a problem. I am getting my shoes. I could make it down, dump, get air, change of scene. I pinch my shoes on. I get the laces in my fingers and thumbs. I lace up. I make bows. Danglings. Nice ones. In the style of pear shapes. People can say, 'You are your own shop window.' I am standing up. My jacket is now on. I am going over to my bin. Careful of being. Good fellow. I am about to bend over in order to lift my bin. That is what I do when, quite suddenly, I lift my bin.

Some of the contents drop, being awful. Easy does it. I can go all the way down, dump, come all the way up. Now I walk to the door. I open the door. Now I go out on to my floor. I go on to my stairs. Now I am going down the stairs holding my smelling rubbish bin. It smells, to be honest. It is my old rubbish. I am descending. Families live in these flats. I need to stop. Let me breathe. I am recovering. My legs are bloody stiff. I am descending again. I take the steps one by one until I get to the bottom. Now I am at the bottom.

I stand in the doorway. I look at the court. I breathe, thinking. Twilight spreads ahead on the court in a wet way. Sometimes young fellows and young ladies walk along. But there are hints of the stirrings of plops. There is not a person. Rain could plop down. Lying at my foot is something. A pink bangle. I have come a bloody long way down. I am the only one who did not know it was dismal. Bloody hell. No point going out in that, I consider. Not even clean air, so why do it at all, I consider in balance. Later is the time to do it. I turn round. I am going back up. I am going bloody well back up. I will have the last of my blancmange. I start up the stairs. Going up, I have to put up with that smell up my nose. It is a difficult way up but eventually I make it with my rubbish all the way up. I have impossible hips. At the top I need to plop down. I get in my door. I must sit. I plop down. I must recover. Breathe in, breathe out is the way.

After a bit I am a bit recovered. Now what to do, I smile. I am peckish, I know. I can resume. Where I left off. Now I get to my feet. I go to the dish by the window. I look at it. I enjoy a yawn. I look out. I can see a cloud the shape of a wisp. People live in these flats, I remind you. A Muslim hates a White. A White hates a Muslim. Why? Change the planet. I make out the powerhouse in that plum-flavoured smokiness. Powerhouses are identical. Here

is a thought. I will share a thought with you. Blancmange in a
minute. Powerhouses have souls. Why not? Souls can easily
hover in airports so why not in a powerhouse? In a second I shall
eat. All things worship God. You take a block like this. Blocks
like Pondicherry Tower can be holy places. Why not? Here is a
mouthful of a word. 'Transubstantiation,' I am thinking when
now, at once, I lift the blancmange. I eat the blancmange. What
do you think? Are you saying we are just sophisticated matter?
Cells. Database. This is what I am asking you. Give me an
answer. I am asking you it. Are you saying I am a fool? Like hell,
friend. Let me get something across very clearly to you. I know
what I am talking about. I am just getting on with my life. Do
you mind? Who are you anyway?

Take you. You have got your own ideas. Correct? You are
entitled. I am me. I am a seperate person. Autonomy. Keep
things civil. Why not? I have my life. I have my pleasures. I pray.
I enjoy the little things. I am busy. I have cleaned the whole flat.
You have to be decent. I work too. I wash my clothes and clean
the flat. A big job. It is not true that I do not work. I work. I
work my testicles off. Pardon my looseness. Language. Outside
things are less moist than earlier. I open the windows. I can hear
voices down there in the night which — it is the shade of a plum.
People are out. Evidence of courting. I can hear loud
footsteps of young ladies. I am a disgrace. This cooking area
stinks. I am on my way to dump my dirty bin, once and for all. I
am on my way. I am getting down those stairs no problem.
Good for me. My lungs. Pulmonary. Careful not to dunt my
knee. It is a long way down. I am not afraid to fall. Soon I will be
at the bottom. I get there.

Now I am at the bottom. I am going out on to the
court with my dirty bin. Breathe the dark. I smell sparks.
That is light abuse. I go slow and take it easy. A must.

Anything could happen. Come on light, perk up. Voices are invisible. I start to walk with my rubbish. The powerhouse hums. This is my chance to get air. Bundles. I walk and enjoy. Up there are grubby stars. Proceed at a civil pace. I could whistle. The point is not why but why not. Accent on the positive. Dump the rubbish. Why not? Temperance. Eat well. I do not choose to go through the tunnel to the back of the flats, preferring instead the long way round and get exercise. The air is heavy on the head. The powerhouse. Cables and bars. Still I walk. A cluster of youths is climbing on an erection. They better not. I will kick their heads in. I pass ignoringly with my rubbish. Bunch of fives.

I walk under the moon. I think: cream moon. I think: slender disc. The moon stays the same as the world is getting increasingly computerized. Bare cheek high above a computerescent globe. I get feelings. I get feelings as I walk. There is cold on my cheeks. Distantly a lorry sounds the horn. Sometimes I get mixed up. I turn round the back of the flats with my bin.

No one is here. It is still. The rotting factory stands behind hedges. Still I walk. I walk and carry. I carry and think. What happens next? I will tell you. Now something occurs. What it is is this. I think I hear a call.

I stop. That affects me. Sensitive. Which I am very sensitive. Naturally my heart is pumping. I hug my rubbish. I look around. It is a mild night. I listen. I see no one. Do you want to know what happens next? I will tell you. I look up. I scan the tower. I see no proof of a call. All there is are smoky leaves somewhere. It is quiet. I notice no one in the smoky quiet. There are so many souls in the tower block, I am thinking when, then, something catches on the heel of my eye. I stare. I continue to. Then, all of a sudden, nothing happens. I breathe out. That was interesting. I turn round. Illusions. I start to walk on smiling as it was interesting. My walking can be like politics. Steady progress. The rise of

China. This was an interesting day. Harvestman. Sweet blanc-mange. Now I come to the big bin. I am there.

I set my little bin down with a little tap. I stiffen up. I lift up the big lid. 'What is this?' I say. But it is full up! Brimful. Brimful of people's dirty stinking crap. There is no room for mine. You must be joking. How am I supposed to dump? Waste products. Necessary. I set down my bin. Take it easy. I stand. I think. I have walked a bloody bit. A hedge shimmers in the breeze. Dumping is a natural rite. Dumping is essential for each and every day. Take an example. I put the lid down again. Bloody hell. Rights of man. I am getting my breath. This is not fair. Is this fair? Take an example. Consider private parts, for example. Why not be blunt. A man's private part fills up with warm milky love. Find no one to give that love and that milk spills out. Must. Cut the crap. Picture the alternative. It going yellowy, curdley, stinking out the part. That does not happen. An unnatural thought. Then the whole would suffer. Do not think that the part is not part of the whole. Dump and be healthy and clean. A car screeches out on the road.

I bend down and lift up my bin. Easy does it. I do not value those screeches. They do not add to the night. I have to take my rubbish back again. Bloody hell. I turn and aim for my flat. This is no joke. I am not in the best mood. To tell you the truth, why am I telling you things at all? I smell my rubbish as I walk. To tell you the truth, I am in two minds about if you are worth it. This plum-stained air is weighing me down. I come round to the court. There are mixed-up feelings in the breeze. Human beings dream. Their grimy dreams are blowing off the concrete of the tower block. I come back to the entrance. The child's pink bangle is still there. It is lying. Disregarded. People do not care one iota. It is in my way. I could crush that bloody thing. I just walk past it. I matter. I go into my stairway. What I do is I just start back up the stairs to my room hugging my rubbish.

There are too many stairs here. Do you know it is easy to meet a young lady round here in the flats? Normal. It could happen. A young lady with good manners could be standing about the staircase at night. 'Good evening,' I would say. She wears black woolly stockings, legwarmers. 'I have seen you about.' She bobs her head.

The stairs are steep. I rest, leaning. Do you say God does not love his creatures? Load of balls. God loves his creatures. My collar is clinging to my neck. It makes me hot. I need advice on how to clean my lino. I am exhausted carrying. I unbutton my collar. I wonder what I should do if this situation with a lady comes up. Be prepared. Let your conscience be your guide.

'Do you know about lino?' I would say. She would come up with me to examine my lino. I am filling up with warm milky love. I restart up the stairs. I would show her into my flat. I would close the door. Switch on the switch. We examine the lino. I can smell her Lifebuoy. She could do with money. I am reaching my floor now. She need not show me her boobies. Simply talk. Share. Inspect the lino. 'Old lino,' I say. Tip. Brush her bottom. I am hugging my rubbish under one arm. 'You are a lovely person,' I say. Healthy and clean. She shrugs. Now I am getting my key out. Warm sticky loveliness. 'What is your name?' I am wiping my feet. I am going into my flat. 'Linda.' I have to get rid of my pool of love. I brush her pear shapes while she looks at the lino. 'No one will know.' I have needs. I slip my rubbish on the settee now. I take off my jacket. I go behind her. 'Now come on,' I say. 'Panties down.' I need to lie down. 'Need your bottom soaped.' This is natural. Nothing wrong. We need happiness. I do not need to tell you my business. Why should I be truthful? You do not matter to me. Irrelevant. You do not love this tower. I love the world. I love her.

———

LOVE MARKS

———————————

EVERY OTHER SUNDAY almost, all through that autumn with its musk-scented rain and those yellow shadows you might have noticed, I caught an afternoon coach into London to see a child. Oh it was so pointless from the start. He needed a real mother, not a mixed-up woman like me. We'd meet on Mare Street, Hackney, in the queue for my bus, making out we were strangers. Ridiculous. Every other Sunday was the same. Until, as the new year approached, it came to an end. And then spring bounced in really sensible and positive-minded. I could nearly hear the birds beginning to cheep, 'Let him be, Jacqueline.' Well those little conservatives would have been right, of course. I'd never doubted that.

One morning I'd got up feeling panicky. I'd been thinking how little I had so far and all that. I'd only recently left someone – a woman, I'm afraid. We'd both been trying hard to make do with it. When each of us realized the other knew we could hardly look each other in the eye. I decided that day to go to London since it was one of the days I didn't work. To take my mind off things. But I just seemed to dangle there feeling left out and slightly weird. All the housewives were out with their squeaky-clean kids in cute new uniforms. There was a strong moon in the sky. Later I happened to run into a young Cockney girl outside a shoe shop near the Angel, one of my lesbian circle. Twice when I'd met her before she was with this wild-looking homeless kid who had attached himself to her. Both times we went into a snack bar, had ice cream and argued politics. I wasn't even all that fond of her, she tried to dye her hair Irish, did herself up like a marigold, looked just as dumb as men would say she was, you know the type.

That day I had a nice tweed jacket and tie on and I couldn't help feeling conspicuous in her presence: you could tell there was this class gulf between us, I had an incredibly bad job and she had nothing. The top of the boy's left trainer was ripped off, he was probably breaking some law simply being dressed so poor. Just to be predictable or to avoid a shower we went to a snack bar again that day. But she was in a crap mood. And she was pissed off at Robbie. Which was unfair, he had problems.

Soon a dispute developed. 'I'm not getting myself in trouble over you,' she spat at him. He frowned at his dish. Basically she wouldn't put him up because the law was after him. I didn't really know the facts but I didn't support her. I didn't say anything, I just kept dipping my finger in the ice cream and feeling unreasonable for doing it. You could hear him breathing. At last she stood up, reassured us how little anything meant to her anyway and flapped out. He blinked away light in his eyes. He was quite tough-looking, about thirteen. He wore a little ink spot on his cheek. I handed him a Kleenex. 'In case you want to blow your nose,' I explained. Everyone was glancing at us, the way we looked, I suppose, they probably thought I was coaxing him to be gay or something. I bought him an another ice cream and said everything would turn out good. I meant I was going to do my best . . .

One particular Sunday – I hadn't been meeting him long – we'd got the bus, as usual without talking. We got off, started walking along Navarino Road past that junk shop beside the takeaway. It sold grinning fish, a hairbrush on a claw, and a whole collection of those stupidly unnatural paintings, perhaps you know it. There was a smell of fireworks or spookiness, or was it just Hackney? When we came to the grocer's shop on the corner we spoke for the first time.

'We'll need milk.'

'Get us a Coke.'

'You stay outside.'

'Coke.'

I nipped in. A doubled-up, knotted woman greeted me with what actually looked like approval. It was amazing she was still on her feet. She was even more elderly and yellow than her window-display toilet rolls. I bought some inessentials: bread, ham, fags for him, milk, one packet of crisps, another lighter, one tin of Coke, a tomato in case. When I came out he was across the street scrounging another fag from an ugly man in a threadbare bomber jacket, stocky, oddly small beside a hedge. I was almost going to walk away. I passed them, ignoring him, until he ran up to my side. I gave him the can.

'Thanks, you're a real friend.'

Those London features of his! — free and mischievous like an eccentric mechanism. As for me, I had the casual face of a ventriloquist as we walked. I asked, 'Did he approach you?' Well I was anxious for him.

'What you mean, *approach*?' He slurped. I could hardly believe any of it. Coughed mist, twinkling shards of bottles, inky figures on the walls and roads. I kept asking myself: what do you think you're at? We came to the house. Already starlight licked about the bins. I lifted open the narrow gate. 'Quiet going in, Robbie.' High above the rooftops, three, four times higher, a newspaper was flapping.

We clopped all the way to the top floor. With a flexed face, I opened the deadlock and let him in ahead of me. 'This room!' he said. He lit a fag. I started making sloppy sandwiches, took the cups, scooped out the blue milk from two weeks before.

It was almost as it was when I'd first come to see it. A little corner room with walls like cardboard, a view of gnawed chimney stacks, skylights, aerials. It was perfect. Later I'd returned with a small suitcase. I'd plugged a kettle in, set two cups out, some plates and cutlery, a toaster, bunged the suitcase in the gross wardrobe that blocked half the window. There was a clapped-out oven on wheels, bedside table and lamp, and that broad, low bed.

He was sitting on it now. I brought sandwiches and tea over. I sat on the gritty carpet. There was a silence. I took a sip. I heard him breathe in. 'So,' I said. 'Talk.' I'd lifted a pack of cards from that corner shop.

'About what?'

I took the cards out. I couldn't think what to say. I shuffled them, pretending to concentrate. 'Just talk,' I said softly. I looked at him. But he mimicked me.

'Just talk, please, I beg you.' I must have looked hurt because he added, 'I didn't say that.' Underneath us someone came in.

'Play cards,' I suggested with a croaky voice. He slipped on to the carpet. He dealt them. His clothes were pungent. He tore up the jokers, saying they were unlucky. We began to play. Gradually a darkness crept over us, aubergine in colour. I didn't know what game we were playing. I watched him pick and flick down cards capriciously. I was ridiculous about Robbie, as if he was like one of those mushy paintings that cluttered up the market in Ipswich where I helped out. He actually had one of those over-drawn innocent pouts.

'Have you got a fellah?' he asked out of the blue.

I smiled tightly.

'No? Tell me.' Below, somebody was sawing something

'Listen.' I spoke low. 'Can't you go back to the home?' He

shrugged. He kicked his trainers off and sat in the most world-weary socks. 'You can't stay on the run.'

'You reckon?'

I looked seriously. 'I'm worried about you,' I told him. 'I care.'

Now his eyes were on mine. He asked, 'Why do you take me here?'

'What d'you want me for then?'

I made a laugh. 'I just . . .' I didn't know what to say. I thought: okay, it's a big mistake, I don't know what I'm doing. At that moment I felt I heard something in the flat below. A loud wince. 'What's going on there?' I said. We listened. It was quiet. I eased on to my feet. I leaned by the window. We looked at each other's faces. I lowered the blind and switched the lamp on. He lit a fag. I crouched down again. His face was thinking about the silence. We held it and smiled at each other. We were waiting for another wince. He bit his lip. A moment later what happened? No, there was no noise. We simply burst out giggling together. I don't know why. We were giggling at the whole situation in this absurd room, I suppose.

He began to show me a card trick. I hardly followed it because my eyes were on him. I watched the tiny trapeze of his features, consonants exploding. We didn't listen for any more ejaculations below. And then suddenly I realized I was touching his shoulder. I got up and moved. 'You see if you were ever found in here, Robbie?' I whispered as he shuffled. He raised his eyebrows, opened his mouth. 'You know I'm not trying to put ideas in your head.'

'What ideas?'

'I mean you're free to do what you want.'

'Pick a card,' he said. 'What is it?'

I took one. 'Knave of Spades.'

He concentrated with his eyes closed. 'It's the Knave of Spades, innit?'

I showed him an apologetic face. 'No, it's not.' We grinned at each other.

'Oh I know then, it's the King of, what you call them ... flowers. Right?'

'How did you know that?'

He tutted. 'The appliance of science.'

The next time I was with Robbie we were lying across the bed looking out at the bruised clouds and chimneys. Dusk was seeping through the glass, it was sellotaped and bloomed olive. And I said, 'If only we could go places together. Without people watching.' He yawned. 'What would happen if the landlord knocked?' He didn't answer. The shadows were taking possession of our bodies. 'I suppose you'd get locked up. I'd be interrogated like hell.'

'Just say I'm your son,' he said impatiently.

'You could hide,' I suggested. 'In that wardrobe.' We looked over at it, a patch of darker black.

'Yeah. Or I could kill myself if you want.' He took out his lighter.

'That's not funny.'

'I could burn myself.' He tried to flick it on.

'Stop it.'

'Why!' He frowned. He flicked again. 'You don't give a toss.'

I listened below and made a gesture to speak more quietly. I sat up straight. 'Can we change the subject please?'

'I'll kill myself one day,' he assured me. A bright flame shot above his fist.

I stood up. 'Well.' I swallowed and smiled. 'I don't know,' I said, 'about you . . .' I closed the blind. 'But I think it's gloomy in here.' It sounded like birds were trilling outside. I switched on the light. He didn't say anything more. I stood at the sink. 'What about one of my specials?' He ignored me. I put my hand on a loaf of bread. 'No?' He was sitting up staring at the lighter. I went and sat beside him. I asked was he hungry. He didn't say anything. 'Don't,' I said, I cleared my voice, 'talk silly.' He was still staring. Poor Robbie. I suppose I should have put my arm around him. But I didn't want to confuse him. I liked him being healthy. I mean, God forbid he should turn out as strange as me. I looked down at his hand. It was mucky. 'Things'll get better,' I said. His fingers twitched. From somewhere in the house an alarm clock went off. 'Can I ask you something?'

'What?'

'Will you show me your hand?'

'What?'

'Not to touch it,' I explained. 'Just show me.'

'There,' he laughed. It was scratched.

'Well,' I said. I pointed at his palm. 'I bet you're going to fall for a lovely girl soon.' He looked at me with his mouth open.

'Why?'

'It's in your palm.'

'Is it?' He examined his own palm. He made little expressions, like dreams. They were like dreams bothered by dust squalls. 'Will she give me a blow job?' I thought: charming! 'That's all she has to do,' he said with a grin. Even so-called innocence is caught up in exploitation, that male stuff. But who knows, maybe he was happy that way. 'I don't want nothing more!' he said. He licked his knuckle.

Once he began to speak about himself. We could hardly see each other in the room. London breathed at the window. He told me his earliest memories of being raised in a place called The Basin by his gran. It sounded almost beautiful so long as I didn't have to live there. Outside toilets. A litter of kids. He loved telling it. An infancy haunted by ancient personalities the family couldn't forget. Some of what he said I didn't even make out, to be honest. I listened to a syllable stream. To reed music. I understood that an uncle died, a child died and his indefatigable old gran proffered humorous wisdom. Never take advice from no one, she'd told Robbie – especially from me.

I found myself mentioning my plain childhood, growing up fairly happily in . . . it wasn't even worth talking about, I said. 'Where?' – he pummelled me. Of all places, I told him, Nottingham, the centre of nothing. Home of Sweetex. I got him laughing. My folks were all right, I admitted. I couldn't blame them, they were straight, struggling. My dad was genuinely sad for me. And now, I suppose, I was feeling sad for this boy. In fact, I felt protective – and I didn't like that. I could understand the concerns of those old harsh judges with faces like withered bollocks. We were silent for a moment. Then he spoke.

'We could live here.' I didn't answer. He tapped my leg. 'The both of us.' I looked away. 'Jackie.'

I stood up. 'What?'

'Can we?'

'No,' I tried to explain. 'It wouldn't be wise.' He pulled his lip. 'You'd attract attention.'

'How?'

He wasn't serious, it was only talk. 'You're just using me, aren't you?' I teased him.

'You're using me.'

'How?'

'I'm fly to you,' he said, frowning at the wall.

Off and on I thought about buying things to civilize the room, as my dad would have put it. I knew it was atrocious taking Robbie up to that high secret square of nothing but shadows and chimney smoke. I had in mind something from that junk shop on Navarino Road, maybe a barnacled cutlass or a stuffed head. One evening I looked in the window when I was killing some time by walking to get my coach to Ipswich after Robbie had got the bus. There was a framed photograph propped on the ground that seemed to have Robbie's London eyes. But then I was beginning to see Robbie everywhere, in babies, I saw an old woman once who looked like Robbie. There was also a deformed embryo. Handcuffs, tentacles that inflated. The worst thing of all I spotted was a joke finger. I walked away feeling stranger and a bit lonelier than before.

One Sunday we sat on the bed frustrated by the room and the empty afternoon. He pinched his penis, taking advantage of the shadows. Underneath us an alarm clock went off.

'Jackie,' he whispered.

'Yeah?'

'Hi.'

'Hi.'

'We've been sat here for half an hour.'

Our own responses exasperated us too every time he farted and I harangued. Brown rain was plopping on the slates. We looked into each other's faces. He lifted his finger and dabbed my cheek for something to do. Eventually, I placed it in his mouth. He put his thumb into my armpit. I looked at him. He lay down.

I brought my face close to his. I bit his eyelashes. His hair stank. He sighed on my nose. After thinking I said, 'Can you do this?' and crossed all my fingers. His face was bored. He stiffened his thumb. It bent really far back, he must have been double-jointed. I was thinking it just wasn't like a real one, it belonged in that junk shop – when there was another noise again.

I shushed him. The traffic hissed below. He scratched his eye. It sounded like occasional slapping or something.

I screwed up my face to listen, but he spoke. 'So am I staying here or what?' He hadn't heard it. He was scrutinizing the walls.

'Listen.' There was nothing to hear now. 'What's going on down there?'

'I'm staying? Nice one.' I sat and thought. 'Unless you don't trust me.'

'I don't like the sound of that,' I whispered. The house was quiet.

'D'you not like this room? I'll do something to it.'

'Be quiet a minute, I'm trying to listen,' I said.

But he swung off the bed. He walked up to the door. He said sharply, 'Let me out!'

'What?'

He was tugging the lock. 'Just let me out!' he yelled.

I shot towards him. 'Robbie, I . . .' I didn't know what to say, I didn't want to inflame him. He was staring at the lock. Then underneath us there began a clear succession of slaps. I made out I didn't hear anything and said, 'What's wrong?' But my voice was cracked.

'What am I doing here?' he mumbled.

'I'm not keeping you here,' I said kindly. I unlocked the door. 'If you want to go you can.'

He shrugged. 'You don't want me here.'

'I do.'

He hesitated. 'Can I stay then?'

I locked the door again. 'Make up your mind.'

He slouched to the bed and perched on it lighting a fag. He inhaled smoke. I didn't speak. Simply for something to do and until he calmed down, I made toast. I stood by the window. I didn't even eat it. I made out the subdued roof and dour windows of what had to be a courthouse standing before a vast spare ground. I didn't know what I thought about this whole situation, to be honest. I was really very divided. I suppose it was only right for me to tell him after a long silence: 'I shouldn't be seeing you at all.' He looked at his trainers. 'I'm not good for you.'

'What?'

'I'm weird, for God's sake.' He tore at a trainer. 'I'm influencing you.' Outside above a smashed dormer window somebody had left some electricity cable and what looked like a cactus. 'Do you think,' I asked him, 'I'm doing you damage?'

He snapped, 'What you mean? Like cruel?'

'Yeah,' I hushed him. 'Am I?' He didn't answer. After a moment I spoke again. 'Am I?' Again he said nothing. 'Robbie?' He swallowed. I thought he was about to speak. But he got to his feet. He let out a shriek. Under his wrist he was holding a flame.

Immediately I grabbed his hand. He was groaning at the top of his voice. He dropped to his knees. 'You're okay, Robbie,' I stammered. I tried to get my hand over his mouth. He rocked back and forward now. He thumped his head with his fist. I tried to stop him. I could hear talking somewhere in the house. 'Robbie, please be quiet,' I said. 'Everything's okay, I promise.' He buried his face in the carpet. I just couldn't calm him. He kept on groaning loud. I stood up. I didn't know what to do. I almost felt like laughing. I walked up and down the room while he wailed. 'Christ, the law will be here in a minute.' It wasn't any use. I leaned by the window waiting for him to stop.

Over time he relaxed. Nobody bothered us from the other rooms. I got down beside him. I looked at his wrist. I said softly, 'What is it?' He sniffed. 'You can tell me.' His ear was dirty. 'Is there something I don't know?' And then I put my arm around him.

'They make you do things in that home,' he said.

I gazed at him. I had to clear my mind. 'What do you mean?' He didn't answer. 'Who makes you?' I flustered.

'What?'

'What do you do?' He lifted his eyebrows. 'Robbie?'

He mumbled, 'Things.'

'What things?'

'Different things.'

If only I could have shown him how much I cared. I brought my face closer to his. 'What kind of things?' I whispered.

He shrugged. 'Clean the windows and all,' he said.

I made something for him to eat. My legs were juddering from all the fuss. Well, a very convincing thought came into my mind now. It was just the sort of malcontentment that suited our oppressors so well, and here I was thinking it. I was thinking how perverse Nature was. Here was a young boy, beautiful on the outside, in hell on the inside. But it didn't matter to Nature what any of us felt, we were just meant to look good. All the injustice and hardship of a person's life, the smell of their poverty, their twisted thumbs, and all the dirt – so often we loved it, the surface expressed it in such a sentimental way. It was horrible, there was something so ruthless about that senti-ment, like we couldn't be truthful in loving, we never really felt. God, I thought, this false world. Definitely the work of an amateur.

When we were sharing my tea he asked me a question. I'd been waiting for it. 'Jackie, have you ever done it with a bloke?' But I couldn't focus on this now. 'Never?' To be honest, I was jumpy from every squeak I heard downstairs. I wanted to think. I could see so clearly how bad his life was, but had I brought him into something much worse? 'How d'you do it with another girl?' I looked around the room pretending not to have heard. In a while he daydreamed as he sat. And I couldn't stop thinking. I could just picture some stocky man below, and some of his most passionate moments down on one knee kissing a severed hand. I couldn't stop myself. I thought about him, and about all the discreet ululation, butchery, amateur dramatics, the zooerastia and general bonking going on in Hackney houses. It was fascinat-ing. In the whole of London, the psychic life glimmering in all those bricks. And it was hilarious, the things I'd heard. The arses that loved eggs. Everyone I knew had said the same thing:

there was every flaw imaginable. Somewhere there would be spinsters chastising their mirrors, some wanker contemplating angels . . .

Robbie was moving his lips secretly. I couldn't imagine what he was dreaming of, but I began to think of a sumptuous young lady, black-clad as a governess whose sole yearning was just to drift down to Pimlico chimneys on an umbrella. Then I remembered the little guy who'd said to a girlfriend of mine, 'Don't be so gentle, abuse me.' And she'd known of a man in love with ropes who just wouldn't take yes for an answer. She'd told me of punters who, strangest of all, were just *into company*. Nobody was normal, I was certain, and almost everyone had one secret, one skeleton. Robbie's friend with the dyed hair knew a woman who'd once asked a bloke to shit on her. I was laughing now louder than anything below.

We did go into that junk shop to get something to improve the room. I had sneaked away from the market one afternoon by arrangement with Robbie, taken a coach to London, changed on it into even shabbier clothes. On the way to the room he had the idea of going in since it was open. I didn't particularly want to in case he broke something. There were some really psychotic things in there. He had a good scream and kept attracting the attention of the man at the counter. There was a pair of glasses for sale. And a pencil case. He mucked about with them. And of course there were some of those weepy paintings of tatterdemalions, as they call them in the market, so absurd. 'Look at that face,' I said pointing one out. We laughed, it was so tearful. And oh, what a fake sky. A white more glorious than anything you'd see in life. I wondered, male propaganda. I'd seen that concocted heaven plenty of times and it was no quintessence of any revelation, I can tell you. It was only a colour, a pale mud. I laughed. God, sublimity was only dirt with pretentions.

Robbie was getting rather fond of a giant moth preserved in a frame. In the end we settled for it, it was an awful-looking thing with one flat side. The man wrapped it up in a paper bag. Working in a place like this, Robbie whispered, must make him really weird. He seemed okay to me, maybe a little bit gay, he looked like a woman who looked like a man. But then again, I thought, maybe he was very odd, his eyes were in the wrong place, like a man badly painted. He could be a proper mockery of fatherhood, he might offer you the plump hand of love that loved to slap. I carried our moth in the paper bag as we walked to the room through fragrance of varnish and late lingering wisteria or something like it daubed on a railing. The police skidded after a car in the distance. We walked holding hands and swaying arms.

On our way up the stairs we heard voices from that room below. Some young bloke yelled, 'Do me a lemon!'

'That nutter,' I sighed as I locked our door. Robbie sat down huffily.

'He's all right.'

'What do you mean?' I said. I sat down beside him on the bed and looked at him long and hard like I was counting spots. 'You say that like you know him.' He got up and sat on the windowsill. 'Do you?' I asked. He raised his eyebrows. I stood up. I hung the moth on a nail already in the wall.

The next Sunday he was upset about something, he sat with glistening eyes. I hadn't bothered to turn off the light. When I spoke to him he simply shook his head. So we were alone with our thoughts. My thoughts were about love. I remembered my dad's view that no one had the love they needed to be healthy, that people were only passing round their damage in the search for it. At one time I'd found this so self-pitying, I'd quarrelled with him, called him life-denying and dogmatized and all the rest of it. But now it had an appeal to me. Everything was physical and left its mark. And this idea suddenly came to me. Even something like love was a pigment on the world's canvas like everything else, not at all transcendental or anything. It looked nice — like those hackneyed heavens — but it was basically grubby, and simply mass-produced. Some love was grubbier than others of course. As I thought like this and as Robbie sat perhaps thinking of whatever he loved and could never get, we looked up at that moth.

I hated it. I began to talk about it, trying to amuse him. I called it Matthew. I said it was like a small ugly fat man. I could see him with this personality of his own: Matthew who lived by himself in the cheapest room in Navarino Road, was really passionate, self-hating, on the verge of suicide. 'Do they have sexual intercourse?' Robbie mumbled. I said he burned candles during the day, boiled suits at four o'clock at night, then went out to parks, frequented flowers, took any young guy at all under his wing. But once they were inside the room he'd burst into laughter at the thought of himself and tear the guy to pieces out of self-contempt. Soon Robbie was giggling unhappily and pinching between his legs. But I wasn't laughing. What would my dad have made of us sitting there? I think he would have worried in case we were just human rubbish, disposable in God's eyes. Well that didn't sound too bad.

One afternoon we'd hurried to the room without getting milk. I needed a tea, I was going to nip out to the shop. He stood by the window obviously preferring the company of his shadow. A bee was battering the window. He had on an old hooded sweater that was too big for him, his cheek was pressed against the glass. 'We've no milk,' I said. I drew up behind him. Dandelions were wagging under a vent.

'Someone's trying to open that window,' he told me.

'What?'

'Underneath us.'

I tried to peer down at the window he was talking about, a small one out on an extension. I couldn't see anything. We searched each other's faces. I touched the neck of his sweater. I said I wondered if the man was really holding someone in there. We went and sat down. It just felt like the sort of irritable day detectives would arrive and shout through a megaphone. Old dears would peer from the gate biting their lips. I stood imagining. I saw us being implicated. 'What relation are you to this boy, madam?' I could see a brute in a raincoat with a bald, circumcised head. 'Friend,' I would bluster. 'Don't give me all that about cookery lessons. We know your type.' 'But I assure you . . . there was nothing . . .' The next thing Robbie would be locked up, I'd be held. I could see it all, my home would be done over, Polaroids of severed buttocks slipped under my pillow in a perfumed envelope. 'Confess!' A fat-mouthed dyke twisted my tit, a rusty lie detector rattled in. Terrible electrodes.

I sat beside him on the bed. 'This is awful.' He stood up. He went to the window. I stood up. 'Look . . .' I began.

'What?' he snapped.

I told him I had an idea, I could nip out for milk and on the way back steal a glance at the window, just to be on the safe side. Because of the mortice deadlock on my door you were forced to lock it when you left. 'I have to lock you in,' I explained as I threw my coat on. 'It doesn't close.' I asked him was that all right. He glazed over.

'Look,' I said, 'I'll leave it open, I don't want you to think I'm locking you in.'

Luffing back from the shop through a shrill wind, I looked up at our gable. The window on the extension was too small, I couldn't really see anything. Maybe it was silly. I didn't know what to think. Between two houses the sun was a very unconvincing brown circle. I clambered back up to the room. 'I don't know,' I laughed, 'there's nothing to see.' I tried to hide a simpering face. But Robbie wasn't there.

I hated myself for leaving the door open. The nutter downstairs could have taken him for all I knew. I locked it. I listened to the room below. It was quiet. I put the milk down. I took my coat off. He wasn't even wearing one. I scraped fluffy mould out of my cup and made coffee.

He didn't turn up next time. I didn't expect him to. But that didn't stop me worrying that something might be wrong or that he'd been locked up in that funny home. We'd talked about celebrating Christmas together, but I didn't see him for the next few weeks so I didn't bother bringing down decorations for the room. Christmas passed. The last day I ever saw him was New Year's Eve. I decided to check the bus stop just in case. And he was leaning against it kitted out in a new jacket and jeans. I went and stood beside him. We were the only ones waiting. We didn't speak, simply stared at a lake that flooded half of the road. Navy clouds floated on it. Soon a bus came wailing to a stop. By the time we got off it was getting dark. I didn't buy anything for him to eat, we didn't feel like talking, we were both just too depressed. We went into the house listening as we passed the room below us. At the top I opened our door and he slumped on to the bed. I washed cups as he smoked. 'Do you want . . . ?' I asked. He didn't respond, so I sat on the bed without making anything. I wondered should I mention the nutter. I didn't hear him below . . . he could have been caught . . . He tweaked his eyelid. The nearest chimney was giving off wisps. At last he said, 'Jackie.'

I folded my arms.

'Would you not try it with a bloke?'

I didn't speak. He didn't say anything more. My heart had got faster. I slipped on to the carpet. To distract from me a little I took the playing cards. I started building a tower. We hated those cards as a matter of fact. I completed two unsafe stages. Then I demolished them.

He sat up on the bed. He spoke again. 'Just tell me, I don't mind.' I fumbled with the cards. 'Jackie?' I looked at him. 'D'you not like it?'

'What do you mean?' I stammered. My arm was against his hand.

'I'm only asking.' He bit his nail.

'But . . .' He was hanging his head, looking at the bed. 'Aren't I more like . . .' How could I explain? 'Sort of like . . . your old girl . . .?' I faded away.

'Yeah.' He didn't move. Then he swung to his feet. He went to the door.

But I called him from the bed.

My head was pounding. I got up. I went and stood beside him. 'Listen.' There was a clamp on my throat. 'Be quiet as . . .' And I lifted my hand towards him. Now I just didn't care any more. He was watching me. Suddenly, I touched his cheek. I was reeling. I could hear my voice. '. . . as we're going out.' I was stroking his cheek. 'Okay?' His tongue peeped out.

'Okay,' he whispered. I took my hand away. Then I opened the door. We went out. There was no one around.

We started walking to the bus. The night was calm. There were petals of something on the pavement. I waited with him at the stop on Navarino Road. 'Sunday two weeks?' he said. I nodded. People were getting into taxis. 'Can't I meet you next Sunday? I'm free.' A bus was coming. 'When?'

'When what?'

'What day?'

I simply raised my eyebrows.

He grinned. 'Sunday after next, right?' He got on and I nodded to him at the window.

I walked back to the room. I'd nearly said to him: Be careful who you're with, Robbie. Be careful of weird people like me who want to get to know you. Inside I gathered the kettle and toaster, the two cups and plates and the cutlery, whatever tea was left, the moth from the wall, the playing cards. I pulled the suitcase now wrapped with fine fluff out of the wardrobe. Everything fitted in it. It was quiet in the house. I left the key on the oven and the room door lying open. I carried the suitcase all the way down to Mare Street to get the coach to Ipswich. It was such a bright night. The clouds were ridiculous.

———————————

AT FREEFORM JOE'S

———————

WELL ALL MORNING I must have been suffering from the hottest stink of my life because when I woke up on the floor there was a big old boot almost in my mouth. I sat up fast. Clouds had got into the room. It must have been lunchtime and it was already dark. FJ was picking stuff off the floor. I leaned on the TV and nearly puked up a black feeling in my guts. He just kept picking. He moaned as he picked like he was a sky disgusted with its feet. FJ is tall. FJ stands for Freeform Joe, a reference to his illness, but he's a smart guy who sits in the flat all day and reads books. Maybe a guy like him could help set me straight, maybe stop me being in love with a girl from this heavy area who can't notice me, for example. Maybe that was my motivation for moving in with him a few weeks before to Grattan Mansions, a gloating red palace of squalor where a thousand families feud and get jumbled. Up in FJ's flat you do everything freeform-style: eat noodles with a pencil and pen, butter bread with a letter opener, crash out under a magazine. FJ is an intellectual. He sometimes alarms you and can sometimes cheer you up. A couple of days ago I'd asked him where he thought the world was heading and he processed my question with two blinks of his telescoped eyes and said, 'That's something we could try and find out.'

'Could we?'

'Anything's possible.' He winked.

So the first thing I said now as I looked among the cans for a speck of beer was, 'Are we any wiser?' His face creaked like he was on acid and if he indulged a proper sneer his teeth would all fall out like dominoes. FJ sometimes clams up inside these minimal responses as if to pretend he doesn't have to leak all over the room if he doesn't want to and has fixed views he can keep to himself. Just sulking? I couldn't get a drink and the way I felt I had to lean against one of those clouds. FJ's most fixed view right now is that Europe will be one big Islamic state one day. Could be. It probably will happen and it probably won't. In fact I'm certain it might. He says there's going to be an ugly war between the light and the dark he won't relish. One time he speculated Britain into war with the USE over sovereignty. But he had just done a load of hash on hot knives when I heard him say that, so that's irrelevant.

I dropped on the arm of a chair and tried him a different way. 'So what happened with Nicki?'

'This is it.'

I considered this evasion a close of subject and knocked on the TV. That was a really big boot, what was it doing here? 'This . . . is . . . it,' he repeated slowly, heavily, like he was sulking down three steps. FJ had been lusting after Nicki of the bird face. And when I'd picked his brains on the state of the future world those couple of days ago it must have clicked in his freeform head how he could get Nicki to get into her nip. Nicki knew Cyn. Cyn's thing was she was a witch.

FJ had said to Jela and his mate Chiken from the mansions and Lora and Nicki and Cyn that the flat was there, free to be used if Cyn wanted to show what she could do. She'd instructed FJ and me to make preparations and left us a big bag of crap. We were supposed to have black bread and grapejuice for breakfast, sort of preparing ourselves for a sacrament of emptiness and despair. We'd just rammed it down the rubbish chute. FJ was to tear open the old fireplace and push the furniture back and sprinkle these ashes everywhere in the room. This he had done. Later when the pubs closed people had started arriving. We were having an okay party, we'd got a crate of cans in and somebody said they had speed, a delicacy. FJ was trying to chat up Nicki in his inimitable style: 'I have a great capacity to talk, because I allow myself to, I enjoy it, I find it good for me ...' Jela was mean with his one joint. Lora's sister who I loved hadn't turned up. Then Cyn arrived in black jeans and a white face and actually smelling of rotten meat, maybe imagining a corpse might propose, or else it was just her regular perfume. That made everyone sober up and they'd swallowed their smirks and said, 'Have a lager, Cyn,' and, 'Just tell us what to do.' 'Yeah, tell us what to do, Cyn,' Jela had said with a smile and she puffed up her eyes at him and squirted psychic liquids to dissolve him. FJ quickly lit a saucer of white wine. I remember the light going off, we all started to strip, people were groping each other. I remember Jela's horrible hard-on. Cyn chanted to herself in a voice which tried to imitate the jealousy of snakes, the crash of waves on rocks, the filth of our flesh. I remember FJ's lenses blinking on Nicki but I don't remember Nicki naked. I remember the pink dents round Lora's waist. I remember Cyn standing with a child's chest, protruding shoulder blades and, for a diabolifuge, a twig in her hand as she squealed, 'Will somebody bleedin' light this?'

'That was some night.' I had to laugh now and I examined the damage in the room. I sighed invisibly at the image of Nicki and Lora and the thought of Lora's elusive sister. A damaged face was reading the news now on TV.

'Yeah,' he said. 'But it's not being able to remember it that keeps me baffled.'

'It's the smoke in here,' I said. 'I'm spaced. Open the door.' Cyn had really violated the light in this flat, it was light with lots of dark sides now. And I thought: it's like light that had a really bad childhood. I got up. I stepped over that boot to open the door myself. 'I was hoping you'd remember,' I told him. I propped open the door with a glass. I wanted to know what we'd done and what I'd swallowed and I wanted FJ to describe Nicki's nervous tits to me in about thirteen sentences like he can. Nicki had probably peeled off every last inhibition. And forced on all of us astral blow jobs. And we couldn't remember because Cyn had slipped us a potion of forgetfulness, the soul of a flea in a silver bead. Yeah. And the voice of a dead man had maybe broken through, rattling the room, bawling: 'Who the fuck's conjuring me up! Jesus Christ, all that Dark-Age-religion stuff is over. 'Cos your technologies are gonna prove us spirits, right? Get yourselves one hundred per cent reliability in simulated feeling, OK? If it reports, say, out-of-machine experiences . . . hello? . . . hello?'

What am I going on about? Don't listen to me, I'm confused.

'What about going out?' I said now to FJ, because I had in mind that I wanted to breathe. 'Get some air. Is that possible?'

'Unlikely,' he said.

'But anything's possible, right or wrong?'

'Right,' he said, and puzzled. 'Or maybe wrong – anything's possible.' He grabbed his jacket. He made himself into an S and glided through the doorway.

'Load of bollocks, wasn't it,' I sniffed as I pulled the door behind me and followed him down the steps and out of the mansions.

Outside there were stains on the clouds. We crossed the court. A colourful sweet paper was fluttering around some broken glass like it was in a panic looking for its friend the peacock. We took the little mound that led up on to the road. I was still not right and my nose smelled ill. Behind the afternoon there were dark blotches like invisible rain sacks swelling. Maybe,

I thought, it's my damned guts taking the form of a dream of streets.

'You didn't notice the anarchist's hard-on, did you?' I gagged.

'The syndicalist?'

'Banana-shaped.'

As we crossed the road a young guy called Mad Eyes watched us from the shop corner. A lonely bus trawled past advertising lips. We joined him.

'F-f-f . . .'

'How's it going?'

'I know what y-yis were up to.'

'Yeah?' I couldn't look at his jittery eyes, blue moons that typed on the day and bumped back every so often like somebody ironing the day with moons or tennis balls.

'A louiggi board.'

'Was it?'

'W-was it?'

'Yeah, we commanded the dead to appear,' explained FJ with tired hatred. I could smell a sea. There's no sea round here, but that's a minor point. 'By the flames of Banal, and the mysteries of the night, and the spookiness of love . . .' FJ can come out with things like that. 'And the lure of the East, and the torture of the Kindly Ones . . .'

'We found out what the world'll be like in twenty years,' I yawned. This young guy just begged to be messed about.

'And the loneliness of Resentful Care . . .'

'W-what's he goin' on about?'

'I don't know.'

'There was quite a lot that got me thinking,' FJ blinked. He turned to Mad Eyes. 'Picture an empty world with no life any more except the people who paid to be frozen at the centre in Electrolux Timepods, and . . .'

'Is it?'

'No,' I said, 'it'll be okay,' and Mad Eyes crimped his lip. FJ's real belief about the next twenty years was something I'd heard him say a number of times: that things were looking up – and down. But he wouldn't elucidate. I had a bet with him to be settled within the first fourteen days of the new century for the value of a hundred pounds assuming 5 per cent inflation that nothing black would happen at all, that we were going into a pretty blanched world eventually. My outline was this: everywhere ending up like Luxembourg, kind of liberal and kind of right-wing. A world terrorist threat from mystic activists. You get air delivered in the morning with your milk. We'll all have jobs. I'd like to work in an eye bank. Or the foetus tissue industry. Pornography will be a social service and bodies without brains will be cloned for this purpose. But I might be wrong. Everything I say might be garbage.

'I would see much more hope in the future for schizophrenics, which is a good thing, obviously – well, that depends – there's nothing wrong necessarily with – this is assuming . . .'

'And you should have seen Nicki's tits,' I said, lamming out at Mad Eyes, expecting him to giggle and drool. But all of a sudden he said something that opened up new dimensions of quantum angelics and electro-evil and artificial ignorance and the speed of fancy . . .

'Nicki's dead!'

'What?'

'She was screamin' out here this mornin'.'

'What?'

FJ was grinning and glowering.

'She was spaced out, she saw a g-ghost!'

Well I got a wave of crap through me. I needed air. A ghost? I had to get to a window somewhere, open a window in the bleak breeze. There wasn't a single car on the road. Now I could hear a squeak. I thought it was a ghost seagull pecking a hole from the other side of the light, but it was only Mad Eyes' brain needing a lubricant. His eyes were bouncing around the sky now: he was giggling.

'So she's not dead,' FJ was saying flatly.

'I n-n-never said she was.'

'You were talking to her?'

'She said she saw a bleedin' g-g-g . . .' I couldn't look at those elastic saucers any longer. 'Down there, w-walkin' past the p-pylon.' FJ frowned and Mad Eyes bit his lip at me.

'How many people were at that party?' I asked FJ. This needed mental attention. But he didn't answer. He was scanning our whole papery, dark white part of the world. I looked in the direction of the pylon. I tried to think: was Cyn wearing big black boots? Or did she conjure up a bloke? It could happen.

'Yeah, I've seen that ghost myself a few times,' FJ was proclaiming, trying to confuse Mad Eyes, complicating life further.

'She was on-on an acid! Gis one?'

'Why do you think that? That ghost's always there, in the afternoons, everyone knows that, dope! Did you think she was on drugs? It lives in that pylon.' But I don't think he was considering this possibility, just nodding at me to get me to verify.

'It does, Mad Eyes, that's its gaff. I know it's hard to believe.' He didn't speak. 'Do you not believe it?'

'No.'

'Why can't you be normal?' FJ groaned. Mad Eyes turned his head away. 'It's a simple question. Are you not normal?'

'We'll show you, will we?' I nudged him. He looked at me with a frowning fish on his face, a complicated fish, actually, that didn't know why it was a fish.

'Yeah.'

'Come on.' I urged FJ to walk. 'We'll go ghostbusting.'

We walked and Mad Eyes lingered behind. I still couldn't

breathe. There was a smell of paint instead of air decorating my thoughts so they looked like dreams. 'Tell me,' I said to FJ. Kids were splashing stones into a grey eye. 'Whose boot was that in the gaff?'

'Whose . . .?'

'I don't believe yis,' Mad Eyes taunted from behind.

We were heading past the flats and down on to the road behind our road. The sky was trying hard not to rain. Anything could happen down here, I thought as FJ massaged his neck like he does when he needs a drink. We could come upon a scientist sitting under a lamppost graffitied all over with formulae. With three presses on a crystal calculator he might announce: Nine times the moon equals a surprise! 'But are there ghosts?' I would shout. He would poke my nose with a pencil: Snap out of it, will you! And I would be left to worry if pylons might be phantom skyscrapers, and there might be always evil thoughts in the air like transparent faces, dead shells, putrid husks from the bottom of oceans . . .

'There it is, down there.'

Now air had clotted into this pylon shape. I was getting nervous. 'The old bill would know about a ghost,' I said to FJ. 'Right? It'd be on computer.'

'Mm?'

'Bugs,' I said. We came to the chicken-wire fence. There was a smell of burning rubber. So far it was okay. So far it was just doing what healthy pylons should do: desiring the sky in a stoical enough way. What was Nicki talking about? She can be too highly strung. You have to hang loose in today's world. Mad Eyes drew up. Inside the pylon there was a kid trying to pick up the ground.

'Let's have a look.' FJ crouched and tugged up some loose wire and curled underneath it. 'Why don't we tell this guy he has to pay his rent?' He walked forward a few steps. I stayed put. He shouted at the kid. 'Get away from there! That pylon's haunted.'

'Crap,' Mad Eyes complained. The kid started walking off, he chucked a pebble towards us. As me and Mad Eyes stood there two people were walking up the road. It was Junior Rat, cousin of Chiken, with Lora's sister. And that's just the sort of additional complication will get me confused. A pin went through me like sticky electricity. Anita had raven-deep hair and black and white clothes straight off a chess board. Why do I get confused? The Rat Boy nodded to me and they walked on. I don't care. I don't care about Anita. But the truth is I love all these streets because of her, that's all. I knew anything could happen down here.

Mad Eyes shouted after FJ, 'I d-d-don't see any ghost!'

And that was when FJ spun round. He sang a high note. 'You simple twit, you believed it!' Then I turned and straggled away. 'He believed it!'

'I n-n-never!'

'He believed it!'

'I n-n-n . . . I n-n-n . . . N-n . . .'

Mad Eyes started after me. 'I n-never,' he said to me from behind. I turned round to him. There was water in his eyes. FJ was trying to squeeze himself quickly under the wire to catch up. He straightened his glasses and stood up grinning an apology at Mad Eyes who wasn't looking, who just mumbled, 'Y-you m-m-mentally handicapped b-bastard.'

'I just find that sort of thing amusing,' FJ said and waved his arms in a freeform way. 'I'm just that sort of person.' I looked away from one of Mad Eyes' tears to the sky in front of us. There wasn't even a bird anywhere.

'What'll we do now?' I mumbled and FJ made a thinking face.

———————

◊

VIII

THE MIRACLE SHED

―――――――――――

THE SUMMER I looked into Cy's teacup and saw pearls we all moved out to the beach. We started kipping in an old lockup shed that was seven fifty a week and no deposit. He'd been planning it. After he'd learned all there is to know about our skeletons and molecules he didn't want a hard job, so he'd goofed around and had got depressed and had to take 'tablets' which he threw away and found Zen. So now he was saying, 'Be still. Discover now.' He was twenty-three, he was our elder. He was going to start fixing up a 1978 2 CV he'd bought for the price of a pair of good runners, see what kind of a job he did on it. Not to sell it, he just loved the idea of recycling a vehicle. I knew he was thinking: I could be a mechanic, I could be happy. Maybe he thought those pearls I saw were wheels. We were glad.

There was Cy and me and Trace and a small guy called Cosmo and a few other vibrations of people who seemed to walk through: Cy's friends and Trace's friends and a man she'd met by being a homeless kid who'd come inquiring about her with love on his face and who we called the Restless One. Cosmo never introduced friends. He was sad — for reasons we got to hear all about when we began to tell each other our lives.

We made the lockup into our home. We scrubbed oil patches the best we could. Cosmo had books on shelves made out of planks and bricks. We grew mustard in tyres and we decorated the walls with curiosities we fished out of skips. I collected interesting details in an old paint tin: hair, bark, pebbles from the beach, tokens from the fairground. These I thought we could exploit rather than use the world up. Cosmo wanted to make us a good home and move all the car stuff to the corners — toolboxes, petrified manuals, Cy's grimy copy of *Zen and the Art of Motorcycle Maintenance*, an antique oilcan and inexplicable things like an old swimsuit and a goldfish bowl full of biro tops. But Cy would always leave a lot lying around. It ended up we just accepted the lockup feel, used balled-up overalls for pillows and would wake with spanners in our sleeping bags. We lived and breathed oil. We became oilfolk. And when we dreamed, oil opened up to us and we understood the hidden world of oil where eels slept their lives away under ooze, where Cosmo said he could see Iranian lorry drivers eating burned bones and gargling with glue.

Late in the morning Cy would start on the 2CV. It had a dented wing and its hood was ripped and the Citroën sign pointing up to Heaven was half snapped off. But it looked cute with bug eyes and a Nuclear-free Zone sticker on the bonnet. Cy would throw open the doors of the shed with us still asleep and work in the yard with his shirt off even though there was no sun, taking it apart to find out how it worked. Soon Cosmo and Trace would get up and I'd get up later when Trace had got back from the shop with borrowed milk and bread. One of the first things we'd done when we'd arrived in this seaside town was go looking for a shop we could borrow from — there was no problem there because in the mornings kids served. Every single item we swore to pay back later on in our lives if we'd money to spare. Meanwhile we had to eat.

We got thumb prints on white slices, we heated tea on a bunsen burner. All this time Cy would be working, disconnecting the splined drive shafts, tapping the drift to knock the king pins out. Or sometimes he'd be talking to people he'd invited round:

real 2CV-lovers, laidback shabby guys who wore eco badges, fleeced jumpers. After eating, Cosmo shaved in the mirror in the car with Cy sometimes underneath it. Then we'd split to the fairground where we had ourselves real jobs. These were good days.

Trace would dissolve. Streets became her. Not even her attendant spirit knew what she did: maybe went looking for men, drank with winos, had Tippex sessions. Her and me weren't really an item, but we'd loved each other from school. She'd sometimes say, 'Would you stroke me?' and I'd give her damp toes fifty rubs and her armpits or the backs of her ears another fifty. At nights in the lockup with Cy and Cosmo there. A few times when we'd wanted to make love we went to the invalid toilet in Burger King off the carriageway.

Down at the fairground Cosmo supervised the flying chairs. He was supposed to take money and strap in toddlers right but any time I saw him he was just standing up looking wrinkled and romantic and like he had sore bowels and really intellectual like a French writer I saw once on TV. I could imagine his voice-over: 'I can but accept my destiny to bear witness to the beauty of dirt . . .' Cosmo walked old and was always complaining of needing operations. Sometimes I'd see him nodding and smiling with old guys of about seventy and that's when he came alive.

Me, I worked in the indoor arcade doing things like supervising the Dodgems. But they were for bumpy flirtations and I didn't gawp. I did my other duties which were: walking about, opening up machines, taking money out, reimbursing well-dressed chancers, stopping kids rocking the Silver Skis. Maybe I was always high on all the oil in the lockup but I saw very varied people walking about: rakeheads, a golf bag, old chipped crockery. People would come out of the Hall of Mirrors worn out and shapeless. And there were also purposeful and unimpressed kids from the flats in scuffed shell suits.

My job offered many opportunities to bunk off too and I pulled myself out of the candyfloss air that stuck smells and whirrs and clobbers and everything together. I'd walk about outside and watch Cosmo across the road near the sand. I'd see the same things every day: bird upon bird, strings of dust on occasional sunbeams, kids sucking exhausted rocks. And I'd hear the waves carrying their message from far away behind wind and water: they said 'emptiness' and 'emptinesses'. One day I went exploring the town, but there were just shops. The moon was in the sky and over a bit from it, almost as bright, was the sun like a glowing ember. There were tea rooms with signs in the window saying, 'No Students'.

Sometimes I'd say hi to French and Spanish kids who got excited and tried out a few words they knew. The only word I knew was *Bienvenido* painted on the Dodgem rink. On their faces I'd see cobbled streets with filthy restaurants and sailors selling onions. And washing lines and bambinos at evening, and pirate ships with black sails moored to the morning. If I wanted a proper chat I'd go into the fortune teller. Madame Star was a fraud. But she wasn't always that. People had more respect when she used to tell fortunes two thousand years ago in Carthage.

Now the only people who ever came to her were foreign girls and housewives from the town. She told the foreign girls they'd marry and have five children. For the housewives she had a different story: they'd be in a bar, it would have pink wallpaper, they'd see a dingy man. The twist was this man would be a millionaire. He'd drive an old clunker around but he'd really have a beauty sitting in the drive and he was going to rescue them from a dull life. She said she had to tell this story because these women just couldn't take in reality.

She said the reality was that we were in the last days. We were the last people. She said aliens knew our world was dying and were trying to help. They'd started to live on our planet in family groups. Governments were providing them with food and news but most people wouldn't find out about them till they appeared on chat shows and talked about their peaceful philosophy and brought a great calm to the Earth. As she talked I wondered if any of those thoughts were the thoughts I'd had when I used to lie in bed listening after my folks had stopped fighting, and if all Madame Star really did was read minds. Because who can tell the future?

I talked to other people, anyone. I tried to talk to the man who sold ice cream who looked like a traveller and like someone who was born of incest and had raised himself and who could never believe in love, just stickiness and being used. He didn't really believe in conversation and said three times: 'I saw you coming out of Madame Star.' I talked to Cosmo. The first time I talked to Madame Star I went and told him what she'd said. He had his hilarious head on and said, 'Nothing would surprise me,' and looked away at trees irked at the smell of chips in their leaves.

Sometimes Trace would appear at the fairground and we'd stand together at a game. She was always bored and had nothing to say and I always wanted to lean over and put excitement on her cheek, but I knew not to because of old people and maybe we'd be thrown out of the arcade. One time we played Derby Day together. She was Gay Lord and I was Saucy Lad and she beat me at every game till I changed to Shy Baby when she lost. I wondered was there meaning in that deeper than we could know. I said we hadn't really played for serious. I said to look at everyone playing the games for serious and caught up in greed. They were trapped on the surface. There were two handsome very American guys standing by the rifle range looking at each other like someone reflecting himself. I said we were wiser than most people. We didn't mind being poor, that was the price of knowing. Trace leaned on my shoulder and said she just wanted to carry on being this happy for ever and wouldn't ask for anything more just in case. Summer looked like it would carry on like this for ever too, just as warm as this and that same greasy rag of sky I could nearly smell every day over the fairground. I wondered did I love Trace. I wondered was she as transparent as the name we gave her and just becoming my colour when she leaned on me.

Cy was making great progress with the 2 CV. He'd patch-welded the chassis, he'd got a hood and a new wing mirror and now he was spraying the body a pale Bon Voyage blue. He didn't talk much about it. He didn't talk much at all. Nights in the shed we sat on seats taken out of the car with a headlight rigged up and we talked and Cy mostly listened. But when he talked we were silent. Only once did he try to explain to us what he called the 2 CV principle. 'Simple elements,' he said with a smile. 'No machismo. No stress. Everything reduced. Light. Functional. So the road is real. In the moment.' Cy didn't have a girlfriend right now, but this car was his girl. And as he talked I thought he liked it much better than any girl. And I remembered him saying once how he had to get away from some woman who made him feel petty because she reflected him small. Now he felt tall. We agreed this 2 CV principle sounded like the right one for the world. But I wondered to myself would there be any world left for it after all.

We didn't use much. In the lockup we had just what we needed, we filled it all up with our talk. Sometimes we got depressed and thought about our death, but, to compensate, little by little we were getting closer. One night Cosmo shared an interesting fact he'd learned. Some guy he'd got chatting to at the flying chairs had told him what a high suicide rate this town had. Just a few days ago some German guy had hanged himself from a bridge. This German had worked it out so that after he died the river would rise and wash his body under the bridge so as not to disturb people: the whole procedure was so Germanic and clean. We shivered and Trace said, 'What's Germanic?' and Cosmo whispered, 'German,' like he found the whole idea an inspiration. Cy said, 'Don't be depressed.' We opened beer and drank out of oily cups. Cosmo said that was okay for a healthy guy like Cy but he knew he was spawned by the Devil. There was silence.

We all knew about Cosmo. We all said he wasn't that, just a natural variation. But he wouldn't have it. He calmed, assured us, he shook his head, he said he'd known what a creepy kid he was from about nine years old. He'd never had a chance to talk about this before. Now he wanted to. It was our privilege. He told us how when he was nine or ten he'd always notice an old guy on the street. His folks would be with him. They would keep talking just as normal while his heart would be bounding after the man. Even at nine, he said, he knew he couldn't let anyone know this. And he could never meet any old guys. He knew too as a kid how unhappy he was going to be all his life long. Just a year ago, he told us, he'd got to know an old guy who'd taken him back. He said how that old skin drove him crazy. They were having drinks. At one point the old guy went into the bathroom. Cosmo couldn't control himself. He had to rush in and embrace the old guy in the middle of the stink. The old guy could only croak to him to go out. 'The way he croaked that,' said Cosmo. 'That was the first time I understood just what I was.'

There was nothing for us to say. We were all impressed by him. This was brave. This was honest. We waited for him to speak again. He said what he really wanted to know was could you be born like him? Was there a word for it? Me, I'd never heard of it before I knew Cosmo. But I didn't say that. Nobody said anything, just kept a peaceful kind of silence. Until Cy said, 'This is the way.' Cy said there was nothing wrong with us that wasn't an illusion, nothing we couldn't heal with stillness. Attend to reality, he said, and we can rebuild ourselves. Cosmo was silent and thought.

We all thought about this. We loved this idea. One night when we were drinking in the lockup I said how in here we could make anything. We could be how we wanted to be. And even if the world was dying we said there was still hope because with all our brains together we could make a new world. If anyone could do it it was us, we could work wonders. We held hands. We cheered. We had spanners. We had nails and spare pieces – a walking stick, an old GEC stove, one of everything. We could use the 2CV principle to build a different planet where nothing went wrong. Cy gave a rare laugh and did a Chinese rap: 'Economical, minimally physical . . .' I suggested a pink, heart-shaped sun that would beat all night in a green sky. We would have clean white sea, we would have crazy, colourful fish flying in the air and bananas on trees and when you got hungry you would just reach up and eat.

Cy said if we wanted to do that we had to start now and not think about the future because the present was all that's real. But I said we had to know if it was going to be or not. And so Trace asked if I would read everyone's cups and pretend to be Madame Star. We had some borrowed tea leaves. She knotted a rag under my chin like a scarf and wanted to paint wrinkles on my face with oil. Cy played a tape of a guitar on a car stereo. Trace sat close to me with a secret finger down my elastic while I read for Cy and Cosmo. She said she didn't want to know the future because what if she was going to die? I told Cy he was a secret womanizer and had lots of girls hidden away. Now he was being reborn and things had never been so positive. I said there was light in his cup and he was beginning to see dawn for the first time in many years. He didn't look convinced and paid me reluctantly with a Dodgem token. I said what's that supposed to be? Robbery. And I put a spell on him to turn him into a seagull. Trace laughed with tears. I really thought Cy could be happy one day and if that happened his life would be more real than now.

When I came to Cosmo he tried to look like he was trying to look serious. I said to have more respect, that it's up to all of us to get psychic to feed the moon. Don't ask me why I said that. But when I read his cup I could really see pictures this time. There was the relevance of trains in his life. Tongs. And a raincoat: someone would be wearing a raincoat.

We sometimes went for walks at dawn. We'd walk along the outgoing tide where air was less warm and used-up and we tried to get that oil out of our heads. The sun was just a circle of ash in the overcast sky. There was no life left in it because people had been shovelling in too much rubbish. The Earth was dead honeycomb under our shoes and it trembled when Trace and I kissed. She said, 'I dare you to touch me here.' So I did. The seagulls came close to us and I thought how old time was and that these were the same shy seagulls with cute eyelashes as a thousand years ago off the coast of Carthage. Carthage, a big sprawling withered flower lying on the street. We four were too refined for this world, we said, we were spirits with only traces of bodies, we were outlines drifting across the sand.

When one morning Cy opened the lockup door and got into the 2CV and suddenly skidded it back towards us we jumped up squealing and laughing. He'd got it going. He had fitted seatbelts in the back and stuck a blue stripe across the windscreen to cut out glare. And I knew right then his old feud with the physical was over because he really was a mechanic. He'd transformed it and that was magic. We were for skipping our jobs and driving it then all the way to St Tropez. But Cy said no, in this town they'd spot us right away driving a non-MOT-ed vehicle without tax. So we waited till four in the morning. Then we all got in. It was a little France itself inside, so we just went for a spin out the carriageway. It lolloped all over the road and raindrops battered the rubber roof. Cy had a tiny Buddha for the dash, which I noticed just by being mindful. We drove up the steep hill facing the seafront past villas with prinked gardens where Cosmo said lawn doctors came running to bandage up after birds. But at the top of the hill there were delinquent sites that creaked. And there were high amber suggestions of houses, abandoned slanted ones with a waste ground behind where we parked and looked down at the town. We drank beer. A seagull landed on the bonnet and Cosmo said it had the same self-conscious glint as the Restless One. They asked me to talk because I was the one who could talk spookiest.

I made up a story for them. I said one evening when me and my brother were kids we came upon an alien caught in barbed wire on a rubbish heap in this burnt-out steelworks. It was looking at its leg in distress because it couldn't understand something as vulgar and physical as barbed wire. Nights in the lockup I dreamed about these fragile ones and now I described how I dreamed them. They are animals evolved to an off-white patch. If you squint you can sometimes detect them shifting between the rain. They get oily hands and faces exploring our shed. They go splashing and diving in oil drops. They steal a look at our blueprints for the new world. They themselves are made on the 2CV principle: minium body, mostly ambience. They have subtle sex. They have the highly developed genitals of children. They want to come to Earth to get back to nature. When we die we become aliens on invisible planets. Now we all looked round at the blurred soaked bricks but there were no aliens to see. Only a smell of smoke. Smoke, I said, was a soul so into itself it burned up and was only able to drift through worlds.

Trace snuggled up close to me and asked where I'd learned to talk like that. I said I was an only kid and used to dream things up. My mum was a quiet person. After a fight she used to sit not talking for weeks and there was plenty of time to think. Trace was relaxed with the beer and now she said did we know what the word 'fairy' meant to her. She asked could she tell us something.

Cosmo had told us a secret and now she'd like to tell hers. We said yeah and Cosmo held her hand. She started to talk about her childhood. She said what she and her sister used to do when her folks were out. Her sister used to tell her a fairy lived down her knickers. Trace would lie on the settee with her knickers down while her sister would look for the fairy. 'You like this, don't you?' her sister would say. She would open the slit and pretend to look up. Every time their folks went out she and her sister would do this. Her sister said, 'You like me looking for the fairy.' She answered yeah. She'd think about how she liked it as she lay on the settee, she'd think about a boy doing it. 'I liked it okay,' Trace murmured. 'I don't know. I don't think I liked it.' Even today she didn't like the sound of the word 'fairy'. Cy nodded and said, 'Confront this, Trace.' Cosmo bit his lip. There was quiet. Then Trace said she wished she hadn't told us. She was crying. We said nothing more. At last we fell asleep.

We woke up in light. We heard cars on the roads. Cy spun into reverse and we shimmied home before all law and order returned. We slept late. We didn't bother about the fairground that day.

It was only ever at night we drove around till Cy MOT-ed the 2 CV and insured it with money his mother gave him. Then one grubby afternoon at the start of September we revved down to the beach with the tax in the middle of the windscreen, leaning out the windows and hooting to attract plain-clothes detectives. We sat on the sand with the car door open drinking wine. The sun was a cinder in a tree top. There was ashy light on our faces. Someone said love your neighbour, and that was our philosophy. The bonds we all had between us walled us in and we talked about personal things in the open air and didn't feel exposed. A lady was walking a poodle and using one of those zimmer frames. Cy said, 'This is a good moment,' and tried to get us to concentrate on now. But right then I was just imagining the end – the sea going still and icy and all the light splintering and crashing to the sand in wicked pieces and silhouettes of trees against a dark sky with silver webs flapping on them. We put some music on the car stereo. It was only pop music. But what was wrong with us hearing it as holy? Maybe people didn't like us sitting there drinking and playing music. But the air understood. The sea understood.

Suddenly Cy leaped to his feet. We looked up at him and then we leaped too when we noticed the 2CV was sitting there with its engine burning. When Cy threw up the bonnet a ball of smoke bounced up above our heads. It was the air hoses, made of concertinaed cardboard, that had gone on fire and the electrics had melted. All Cy could do was throw wine over the smoke and leave the bonnet open. He sat down and we didn't speak. We didn't know how we were going to get it back to the shed. We were sitting there for a bit when Trace reached over and stroked my fingertip and whispered how much she loved me. She said she'd never trusted anyone like she trusted me. As soon as I kissed her Cosmo sniggered and Cy smiled and then we all lay on the sand crushing our sides. But after that I had to tell Trace the truth. I had to tell her how the time had come for me to go. The lockup could do so much for us, it could heal us if we wanted. But I said for me something else was waiting. I couldn't say what. I explained in a way she'd like, I said maybe an alien ship might come and take me away. But meanwhile I had to look. This was hard for Trace to take. There were tears in her eyes and Cosmo whispered softly to her and calmed her. There were tears in my eyes too and Cosmo's eyes were worried as they always were. But I knew they'd all be okay before the end. I could see it. Cy would fix up the 2CV again. He'd be a mechanic and love every moment. He had made himself. Cosmo would run into some old guy in a raincoat and travel across Poland and Hungary at night and live with him till he died and inherit a fortune in a silver trunk and build a men's hostel in New York. As for Trace, she would always have a hundred men to worship her and by the laws of chance there'd always be one she could trust. She understood that I couldn't stay, it was how I was and I couldn't change. And I would always keep on moving because there were just so many worlds to love, so many lives to live.

_____

DARK HOUR

_____

ONE DAY GERA walked in but I wouldn't look up from Lethal Weapon. I was sad because I didn't have money for it. Exhaust got in from the street. He went to the corner. My brother was there in a green shadow at a game. His arse went tight when he banged the buttons. They talked about the game. I stood about, then I watched Gera go. He walked with the chink of new bullets. Cars were jammed outside. I didn't get on with him. A minute later my brother walked out. I leaned against a glass front and watched a game.

When Dano came back home I was sitting with some mates at the dry stream at the flats. 'You're wanted,' I told him just for a doss.

'Am I?'

A picture drifted past my face of my old one trying to snatch air in front of her face. She said if Dano got caught up she would batter him. I had a promise to watch him but that was just a load of bollocks because Dano would kill me if I ratted and anyway I don't give a bollocks. He started going. Then this is me: 'Gis somethin'?'

'I haven't a penny, John.'

'Ah go on.'

'I swear.' He balanced on a bike wheel that was lying there. The warm afternoon made you kind of sick. We watched my mates passing a robbed Walkman. He was thinking. The sky was a black blanket. 'D'you know what I was thinkin'?' he said in a low way. 'D'you wanna make somethin'?' He stepped over the mud. I went with him. 'D'you wanna do a job for us?'

'I don't mind,' I said.

'I'll tell you later,' he said. 'Right?' I bobbed my head. He went on to the tarmac and up to the flats. Then I sat about dossing with my mates. A Honda Civic went by but it was making a lot of smoke.

Later me and Dano crossed the road and leaned on the railing outside Silver Palace. Not as many cars were there. I hung over the railing and tried to yawn in the stillness. 'D'you wanna go robbin' with us?' he said. 'Just come along and watch.' A shadow came out.

'What do I have to do?' I said.

'Nothin',' he said. 'Just trust me.'

'I know.'

I flopped off the railing. We started walking. I wasn't going to trust him. I was just tagging along for a minute to see. We wobbled in bruised windows. Diane and Sharon passed us and he nodded. We walked to the top of the road. We stopped at the old fountain. 'Here?' I said. We sat down.

'He'll be here in a minute. That's him!' said Dano.

'Who?'

'We'll go for a spin, right?'

'Where is he?' We walked along the road until Dano stopped. An old car opened its door. Dano looked round. He said to get in the back. My stomach was a bit dizzy. 'Where are we goin'?' I whispered.

'It's cool. Quick.' I got in and he got in the front. The car took off but the traffic was jammed.

'So,' said the man. It was an old fellah. 'You okay back there? Haven't I seen you before some place?'

'He's kind of shy, you know,' said Dano. 'He doesn't really

know about it. Well, he knows about it . . .' Dano lit a smoke for us.

'We'll just go for a spin,' said the man. 'What age are you?' Dano got the window open a small bit.

'Fourteen,' I said and the man said 'No you're not!' The cars were slow and they didn't really talk and I yawned.

The man pulled the car into the grounds of a church and parked it at the back. He twisted round. He blinked at me and went: 'Well, you see there's . . . I'll tell you the truth.' He sighed. He leaned closer. 'Well,' he said. Then his hand went on my leg. I looked at Dano who shook his head tinily. The man spoke in a kind way. 'Would you be able to tell me . . .' He thought for a minute. 'Can you be a good young fellah?' I caught Dano's eyes again and they glanced away blinking. The man's hand went back and forth on me for a bit and he asked me questions. I had a horn.

'Is this what I have to do?' I asked. The man's eyes looked at my legs.

He went, 'I was thinking . . . Would you like to make something?'

I thought. 'Not really,' I muttered.

He smiled at me. 'A score?'

I looked out the window. There were houses and clouds. 'I don't really want to.'

'Ah he will, Ken,' Dano said. 'The next time.' The man looked all over my face and shook his head. Then his head nodded. Then he went back in his seat in a happy way.

'Home sweet home?' he went.

'Yeah.' The church started chattering.

We started driving. The traffic trickled. He asked Dano was I upset now.

'No he's not. Are you?'

'What?'

'Are you upset?' Dano laughed.

I didn't know so I said to the man, 'Can you get the full clock out of this?'

'Yeah. More.'

Dano went: 'D'you like him or d'you not like him?'

'Like him,' I said. And I added, 'I have another friend now. I'm happy.'

'He knows Gera and all,' Dano told me.

'Do you?'

'Gera's a very good friend,' said the man.

I thought I should say, 'Ah, he's dead on so he is. He has a nice personality, d'you know?'

We were getting near to where we had got in the car. 'You'll do it for him, won't you?' Dano nodded to me.

'When I get to know you,' I said. 'It's just, you're new.'

The man pulled in. Dano said, 'Tomorrow?'

The man nodded. 'Will you do that thing?'

'Ah, it's cool,' Dano cut him off. He got out and let me out. 'Nice one, Ken,' he said and slammed the door.

'Bastard,' I said to Dano as we walked back in the brown air. He handed me a fiver. 'What's that?' I took it.

'For goin' with him, you dope.'

'You said you were robbin' him!'

'I want to rob his *gaff*!' He was loud. 'I need someone with me.'

'Well it won't be me, that's a *fact*.'

'I was gonna explain about him, John,' he said. 'He's a queer.'

'Why didn't you then? Cos I wouldn't have gone, that's why!'

We went into the flats. A tyre was burning. 'Don't flash that,' he mumbled. Dano is a dirtbird and his face looks like a dog.

My old one got me up the next day while I was thinking of the man wanking Dano. She came into our room and said, 'Where's Daniel?' I said how was I supposed to know. I was in a hurry to get out. Everything was all over the kip in our gaff. 'Do I not have clean shorts?' I shouted to my old one.

Here's her: 'How am I supposed to know?'

'Fuck off then.'

I got on my clothes. Then I went out and crossed the road. I just leaned on the railing outside Silver Palace and waited for Dano because I hadn't the money to go in. I was disappointed because it was a gloomy day. I smelled the dust and I was tingling. A minute later Dano came up the road with a can of Lilt. We started walking up to the old fountain. There were Porsches and all parked. I looked at us in their dusty windows.

Dano said, 'Watch him, right? In the gaff. He could try anything.'

'I better not have to do anything,' I warned him. Because I was only going along for the money.

'Don't be stupid! I'll be there.'

'How are you gonna rob him?'

'How do you think?' he said flattening his jacket. I looked at it. I got a bit worried.

We went and sat on the fountain again. There was rubbish in the fountain. I went, 'How much do I get?' but he didn't know how much was there. Our flats were leaning against the sky. The colour of the sky was called buff. The sky was slipping into your head. My hands were grubby. I hated them. I took my comb out and raked my hair. I couldn't get it to sit right. Then Dano stood up. 'Don't make a bollocks of it, Dano.' We walked along by the cars again. 'I don't know about this.' The car door opened. Dano looked round and we got in again.

'So?' said the man.

'The gaff,' Dano said to him. 'If you want. It's up to you.'

The man turned his head round to me. 'Will you do it? Just for an hour?' I didn't speak. 'Eh? Good-lookin'?'

My face was bored. 'So are you,' I said. Dano smiled at that. 'I thought you were gorgeous the first time I seen you.' The man blinked. 'Why d'you have that moustache?' I said. 'Is that real?' The man started the car and started driving.

We drove past old markets that were bricked up. I saw tiles and walls with layers of paint. A bit later he said, 'Not long now.'

'Your gaff?' I thought I recognized where we were. Soon there were big cylinders for gas behind the houses. The sky was muddy. He parked on an empty street. I was tingling and kind of tired of it.

'Now,' he told us before we got out. 'Just don't whisper.' We got out. He took keys out. We stood while he opened a door on the side of a boarded-up shop. A dog wagged its tail. I whispered to Dano had he got the smokes. Then we went in. There were stairs. The man closed the door and we went up into a flat. He locked the door of it. 'Great,' he said and smiled. It smelled of socks. Dano used the jakes. The man poured a cup of milk and asked did I want a drink. His hand brushed past my arse.

'It's cool,' I said. 'Dano, light a smoke.'

I went into the jakes after Dano. I didn't know what to say to Dano. He puffed into my ear, 'Go along with it for a minute. Then you can tell him to fuck off.'

'What?'

'It's cool.'

We both went back in. I was bursting to giggle, then Dano said to the man, 'I was gonna ask you for eighty. Him sixty and me a score.' The man was leaning against a surface. I was thinking if the man kissed me I had Lilt on my tongue.

'It would have to be forty,' he said and sucked his lip in.

Dano nodded at me and went, 'Yeah.' The sun was falling on the surface. The man asked Dano to go into the bathroom. Dano asked for something to do there. The man looked around. 'Even give us somethin' to draw with,' said Dano.

'Where's he goin'?' I said. The man gave him a notebook and coloured pens. 'Why're you goin' in there?'

Dano gave me the smoke and said, 'I'll be in the jakes,' then he went.

The man sat on the bed. My heart started to kick. He asked would I come over. I said what did I have to do. I finished the smoke. He nodded and I went over. He said, 'Do you mind?' He put his hand on my shoulder in a sad way.

'Don't care,' I said and flipped my shoulders. He lifted up my jumper. He pulled it over my head.

'You haven't much on.'

I looked at the jakes. 'Where's Dano?' I asked.

'In the bathroom,' he said in a playful way as he took off my cross.

'Is he?'

'Yeah.'

I nodded.

'I'm just the luckiest man in the world,' he said. 'You know that?' The cylinders were close to the window. He sat me down and lifted my foot on to his lap and took off my runner. 'Smelly feet.'

I asked did I have to get stripped. He had a pimple on his neck. He pulled down my tracksuit bottoms. I went along with it. I had a big horn. I said I was a bit nervous. His hand went back and forth on my leg again. It was cold.

'What's your name again?' he asked.

My tongue made a tutting noise and I went, 'Nobody.' With a smile he asked could I come off. 'What?' I said.

He stood me up. 'Turn round,' he said. Then he pulled my shorts down. I was afraid of someone coming into the gaff.

'Dano won't come out, will he?'

He shook his head and patted his knee. I had to go on his lap. His fingers went up and down twiddling me. He gave a big sigh. He said how cream my legs were. His hand was grey. The lace curtain put a shadow on it. He said I could come every day after school if I wanted. 'Is this it?' I said. His other hand rubbed my back.

'Have you never done this before?'

I said, 'Yeah.'

'Dano said,' he said, 'you knew about it.' He pressed my nose. I sort of felt sorry for him. 'You don't?'

'Do you like sex?' I asked. He closed his eyes.

'Like it?' He was at my dick again. His throat swallowed. He shook his head. 'I . . .' he said. He stared at my face. He made a soft laugh. 'I fucking love you.' It went quiet.

'I love you too,' I mumbled. I heard my stomach. I needed a piss. He was wanking me too much. I was afraid of pissing on him. I was going to ask him to stop. I was going to ask if Dano did this with him. Then all of a sudden I got a thrill all over. I heard him breathe, 'Good boy.' My head was kind of against his arm. He stopped rubbing my dick. I looked at it. 'What's that?' I said. He pulled me close. 'Is that my spunk?' I said. There was a nice smell like rubbish from outside. He was looking at me. He used a tissue and wiped it off my leg. He rocked me on his knee for a bit. 'Can I go now?' I said. He pressed me closer.

'Well I . . .' he said.

The curtain was twitching. I jumped up. 'Will I get dressed?'

He watched me start to get dressed. 'Could you not . . .?'

'What time is it?'

He got up and grunted, 'Okay.' He came back with a tenner and scratched my leg and smiled. He put a finger on his lips. He whispered, 'Don't tell Dano.' I took the tenner and shoved it in my shorts. He went into the jakes. It was bright and we could go and play loads of games. Dano came out. I was a bit embarrassed.

'Where's me stockin'?' I said in a messy voice. I didn't look at him. The man came and took his keys.

'Youse ready?' he said. I tied my runners fast. Dano put the notebook down. He had drawn a young fellah sucking a big nodger. The man tore the pages out and stuffed them in Dano's pocket and said, 'You know not to talk. Or whisper.' I remembered about my cross. When he was sure we were ready he opened the door and we went down the stairs and outside. A milk top blew along. Then we got into the car and drove home.

When he stopped the car he said, 'Can I see youse next week?'

Dano said, 'Yeah.' He handed Dano forty. 'Nice one,' Dano said and opened the door. We got out into the woozy light. We gave a small wave as the man drove off.

On our way to the amusements Dano didn't say anything but I said, 'I'll get him shot.' The traffic fumes were kind of sweet. I said give me my money because I was broke. Litter was twitching on the surface of the road. I took a piss behind a billboard.

I started spending my tenner and Dano didn't know. I was going to save something for my old one but we were pouring it into the machines. We were happy in the amusements. We were standing in the green light banging the buttons when Dano said with a shrug, 'There was nothing to rob . . .'

I went, 'That's life.'

'Don't start goin' up to that queer on your own!'

'Fuck off, I won't,' I laughed.

x

—————————

NATURALLY STRANGE

———————

MY MA AND I went over the bridge. The sky was a purple wash. Down on the quay my ma made out furniture sitting out. One of her fingers was in my pocket. It kept me at her pace. The horizon was brown. She had the address of the flat and it wouldn't be far to it once we got beds.

The quay was jammed with steamed-up buses. Stars were out. Queues were merging into each other. I decided to walk a bit slower than my ma now. Her finger was strong. I caught a glimpse of mirrors and plants through the bodies. Small twins were messing with the mirrors. A man came out. They hopped away. He lifted the plants in. My ma looked up at me. She clutched her purse. 'Here we are,' she braced herself. 'What's it to me?' I mumbled. She jostled in after the man to ask about beds.

I strolled in and stood near the door as if I was browsing the old cabinets or the old tellies. 'This one?' she called to me brightly. 'Nice,' I said without turning. I heard her say, 'How much does this cost?' The man walked up to her. 'It's not, is it?' I heard from her. I drifted out of the shop into the crowds by the river and stood there. A woman was fat. She was all boobs. She stood back against the glass of a sweet shop looking sad and booby. Her feet were in a pair of runners. She looked at me when my ma came up and said, 'Paul, hurry up.' The man carried a bed up. He set it down in the wet mud. His face was splattered with freckles like the mud or muddy stars or tea spilled. He said, 'There,' and went inside with mirrors. I went near my ma and held the bed. I looked from it to her. The iron frame was rusty. The mattress had a tea stain. We stood not speaking. The crowd was very pushful. The man came out of the shop again and slid a metal grid down from nowhere with a crash. At last I said something.

'Only one?'

The woman was still there. She made me think of a date. She hugged a doll in a box. I said again, 'One,' to my ma. My ma would hardly fit there. There was a brown smell from the river.

'Oh?' my ma sighed. In the crowd I saw the identical kids again.

'Well?' I said.

'Will we throw it away?'

'Good idea.'

She lifted the bed on to her foot. We started to shamble through people. The bed blocked my sight. I kept kicking her big ankles.

As soon as we turned off the quay the way was clear. The purple sky was all around the street. At the foot of a hill we laid the bed on the ground and shoved it up past foggy buildings. The castors roared and squeaked. People watched. Some buildings were sliced right in half and kept from toppling by giant props. Kids stood at a corner twitching and sniggery. A church sounded from far away. We rolled into the lane we were looking for called Mary's Lane. Walls came close. All over the ground was squashed fruit. Someone threw a pebble. It began to rain as we stopped at a door facing a big old market. My ma opened the door with a key. We jerked the bed through the narrow passage and managed it up the staircase to the flat.

At the top of the stairs my ma was very flapped. We leaned against the walls. 'Is that it?' I asked nodding at a door.

'Yeah,' she panted. 'Flat four.' There was a smell of a wet coat or a wet dog. 'So,' she said. She took out a key and tried to slip it into the lock. It jammed. She pushed the door hard. It opened. 'Let's have a look.' She went into the flat. I left the bed against the wall of the staircase and followed her in.

The room was small and old with a wardrobe and a chair. I looked around it. There was more of a smell. The wallpaper was a dingy lime. There were no other doors. There was an oven beside the sink. 'This is just one room,' I said. My ma grinned. I squinted round the room. 'Where's my room?' I said. Her face got twitchy. 'The bathroom,' I said. I went to the window. The city was like a cut-out of roofs and copper domes. Behind me I felt her taking off her coat and folding it over the back of the chair and she sat down.

'It's only for a bit,' she said. 'Till I get money. What do you think?' I put my forehead on the glass. My breath steamed it up. I didn't turn round and she didn't move for a bit. At last I swung round and said, 'Well, I'm not living in this dump,' and walked out of the room. She called after me, 'Oh no now Paul!' I didn't know where I was going to go so I stopped on the second stair.

'What?' I snapped.

She came to the doorway. There was water in her eyes. 'Try,' she said. Her lip twickered.

'Why can't we go home!'

She pulled a face at the ceiling. Her eyes were bigger than I thought. She sighed, 'Christ.' She came and stood beside me on the second stair. She reached her arm round my shoulder and whispered my name. She snivelled. She said my name again. I didn't acknowledge. Then she said very quietly, 'Look, Paul,' and paused. 'You know the way . . .' I was peering down the centre of the stairs to the ground. 'The way you always wanted a brother?' She started to rub my shoulder. I flicked it.

'No,' I said. 'When?'

She rubbed again without saying. Then she said, 'I need you

to help me.' I mumbled to myself the word 'dump'. She dropped her head. I thought for a moment that she was beginning to burst out crying. I wasn't looking at her so I wasn't sure. I didn't say anything. She lifted her head and I heard a snivel. It got me tense. I turned round then to her. Her face was ugly. I tried to swallow. 'Okay,' I said.

She spoke softly with her eyes on my chest. 'Will you try?'

I examined my stair. 'Yeah,' I told her. I smiled. I turned and walked into the room. She came after me. She sat down. 'It's not that bad,' I said looking round. I kept my smile. 'It's good,' I said.

She said, 'It'll be good, you'll see,' and dried her eyes. She smiled and flittered her eyes.

'The wallpaper's nice,' I said. 'Old-fashioned.'

She said to me nodding, 'We can buzz here together,' and got up again tiredly. She started to fill a kettle with water. The tap spat.

I mumbled, 'Can we.'

'Tea. And then we'll bring the bed in because . . .'

That evening I sat on the wobbly chair by the window thinking why we had moved to here. The room filled up with the purple sky. My ma cleaned. She carried up bags with our clothes and things in them from where the owner of the flats had been storing them for us in his flat below us. She carried a fancy gas fire up to the room. Then she carried up a canister of gas. She brushed down the mattress and covered it with a sheet and did the bed. I drew the curtain. On the mist behind it I wrote 'dump'. I wiped over it. Soon my ma got a pot. She said, 'You're having eggs.' I went to the bed and sat on it for a change. I couldn't get used to the room. It was too gloomful for me. It was cold. I decided to say something.

'Do I not get my own room?' She stopped still for a moment. She put eggs in the pot. 'It's just,' I said, 'I need one.' She turned on the gas.

She said softly, 'Do you not like it after all then?'

'It's bang on,' I told her. She stirred the pot with a spoon. The gas hissed. 'I just need my own room.' She didn't answer. She shook the spoon dry. 'How am I supposed to play tapes?' She took another egg. The gas was loud. She put the egg in the pot. A moment later I said, 'Why isn't there a telly?' Suddenly she slammed the spoon down.

'Listen to him! Telly! Play tapes!'

My shoulders jerked. 'So what?'.

'Why look at me?' she said. 'Why can't you get some money? Get a job!' She pointed at me with an egg. 'It's you that wants a telly!'

I stood up. 'I'm going out,' I got my shoes. I sat on the edge of the bed and put them on my feet.

'Where?' she said, clutching her hair.

'Anywhere.' I rummaged in a plastic bag for my coat. She turned the gas off. As soon as she had got her coat we walked down the stairs and out on to the lane.

We walked round to the flats where we were living before with my da. My ma wanted to call into my auntie. When we got to the flats I told her I would catch up in a minute and I went on my own in the side entrance to see my bird. Clouds were passing behind the moon. I went up in the lift and knocked my bird's door. She opened it. 'Can I let Paul in?' she asked behind her. 'Don't get in my way,' I heard from her ma. My bird stood back. She had her hair in a bouncy pony-tail. I went in. Her ma was ironing in the room. There were toys on the floor and rotten flowers in the corner. We sat over near those. The telly was on and her baby brother was babbling in the other room. She took my hand. 'Well?' she whispered. 'Tell us.' She had a wart on her knuckle.

I cleared my throat. She waited. 'Tell you what?' I said with a quiet voice. She squeezed my knees and made them jump. She told me to stop messing. I glanced over at her ma. 'I don't know,' I whispered. 'It's a really small gaff.'

'Doesn't matter,' she told me. I didn't answer. I peered out of the window. Trees were stirring behind the flats. For something to say I said, 'How's the flowers?' She said 'Okay.' I asked what the wart was on her finger. 'A wart,' she said. 'I'm raging with it.' She bit it. Her ma went into the other room. Then she said, 'It doesn't matter how small it is.' She gave me a sexy look. She took my hand again. 'Does it?'

'No,' I answered her.

'A bed's all we need.' I was horny. 'Isn't it?'

'Yeah.'

She stroked my thigh in a playful way. 'So?' She sat back.

'Swear you won't laugh then?'

'At what?'

'Our gaff.'

Then her ma came back into the room and we stopped talking. We sat close on the settee for a while watching telly until her ma said, 'Samantha.' I pulled my lip. 'It's getting late.' We both grinned.

'I'll see you, right?' I said jumping up.

'When?' She came with me to the door.

'Tomorrow.' We stood outside and kissed by the lift. I smelled chips in her hair. There were yells echoing in the tower. My hands held her waist. She squirmed. I lifted her blouse. She touched the lift button. 'Are you coming in?' I said. The lift opened. She said, 'Your arse!' and stepped back. I got in. It smelled of piss. I said, 'See you,' and gave her a leer as the lift door clanged shut.

The door on Mary's Lane was open. The door of the room was also not locked. I pushed it. The light was off. My ma was in the bed. The room smelled of her. She was staring at the bulb on the ceiling. She didn't move. I forced the door closed as far as it went. I went and sat down quietly on the chair. A chilly wind came through the window. She still was staring.

'Were you all right on your own?' I asked. She just moved her eyebrows. I sat for a few moments. There was a shout in the flat below. I asked, 'Where am I going to sleep?' At that she rolled over and faced the wall. I took off my sweater. Then I took off my trousers. 'Well,' I said, 'I'll get in.'

'Get in,' she mumbled. 'It's warm in.'

I went over to the bed in my Y-fronts. 'Sorry, I got talking.' She didn't respond. I climbed into the bed. It made a groan. I shifted to the edge to avoid touching her legs with my legs. A spring from the bed was sticking into me. I couldn't get used to the bed. I tried thinking about Samantha and I saw her pointy tits. I got a hard-on. There were dark barks on the street. I tried to wank a bit lying on my side without making any movement. A leaf was in the room.

It was cold when we woke up next morning. I said 'Hi.'

'I just don't want to move,' she said. There was sun spilled on the quilt. She turned her head to me. She put on a sore face. 'One, two,' she said smiling. Then she crawled out of the bed. She snapped on the fire and leaned on it holding her stomach. She filled the kettle from spurts from the tap and put it on the gas and opened the curtain. She went out to the toilet on the floor below and I swung out of the bed and pulled on my jeans fast. When she came back in she said, 'We have to go out soon. After toast.'

I peered out. Spires came right up to the window. I said, 'Where?' and she went, 'We need more blankets from home. Stuff. Things.'

'Why have I to go?' I said.

She grabbed her big dress. 'Right,' she said. 'Let me get

dressed.' She opened the door for me. I went out. She closed it behind me. I stood by the door waiting.

'You know what we need,' I called in. 'Cheer the flat up. Ornaments. Things. Fruit. Make it nice.'

She whipped the door open. 'What do you mean? It's a palace in here. Are you coming in?'

'No thanks,' I said. I went in. I took the steaming kettle off the gas. 'I've to go out.' She stood still looking. I put milk in a mug.

She said, 'What?' I drank the milk. 'Where?'

'Somewhere.'

'A secret?' She frowned.

'Yeah.' I put my shoes on. She sat down on the bed. I poured more milk.

'You need to take the fire down and the canister,' she told me and lowered her eyes. 'For me.'

'What?' I drank the milk. She said that the fire was from downstairs and that we only had it in the evenings on loan at the moment. I put on my jacket. 'Would you take them down?' I asked. I went to the door. She looked at me from the edge of the bed.

'You needn't think I'm doing everything!'

I pulled my lip. 'I won't be long.'

'I don't feel good on my own.'

'Five minutes,' I said. I went out.

The sky came right down on to the lane. Men were hauling boxes from the fruit market. I could smell manure. I walked over to the flats to see Samantha. There were nests in the bare trees like big gobs. When I got there she opened the door. I went in and we sat around her flat with her ma and her baby brother. I told her that my ma was maybe about to go out. A bit later we walked round to the room on Mary's Lane in order to cuddle on the bed if my ma was out. It was raining thinly. She carried a bunch of flowers she was going to sell later on in town. Near the lane there were buildings bricked up that called them 'Roman-looking'. We grinned when we came to the door. I kicked an orange peel from in front of it. I knew my ma would leave the door open for me. We crept up the stairs. Outside the room I listened. There was no noise. I pushed the door and went inside and she followed me. My stomach was jumpy. Our shadows were on the old-fashioned wallpaper. I shrugged my shoulders. 'In here,' I said. She was looking around.

'Is this it?' she asked.

I said, 'On that.' I walked close to her.

'Whose bed's that?' she said. I touched one of her tits. It was stiff. I was dying to get into the bed with her. She twisted away from me. She set her bunch down on the chair by the window. 'Where's your room?' she asked. My face screwed up. I walked over to the oven. 'I'm not lying on that,' she said. I felt stupid and I made for the door not thinking. 'It's probably got disease!'

From the staircase I saw my ma was coming up the stairs. Samantha came out. My ma managed it to the top carrying food in her string bag and saw us.

'I just . . .' Samantha started brightly, 'brang over flowers for your new room.' She skipped past my ma and down the stairs. 'So I'll see you, Paul.' My ma went in. I glowered down at Samantha over the stair rail. Her wobbly arse was bouncing away.

In the room I said to my ma, 'Did you go out?' She shook the rain off her hair.

'No,' she grumped, taking off her coat.

'You never bleeding go out,' I said in a smiling way.

'You be bleeding careful what you do to her.' She picked up the bunch of flowers. It was colourful. It looked expensive. I looked in her shopping. 'Are these for the room then?' she asked.

I didn't answer. I said into her shopping, 'What's it like being a stupid person?'

All she did was go, 'Is this bouquet for us?'

'Mm.'

'Don't you go and do something stupid.' I took an apple. She set the flowers down. It was lots of different colours and flowers. She went to the oven and boiled a kettle and took out chicken. I sat on the floor and ate the apple. The next thing she said was, 'Would you be able to look after a baby?' She reached a mug of tea over to me.

I said, 'No, course not.'

She went back to the chicken. She brought pieces over to the centre of the room. She got down on the floor. I reached for chicken. 'That's not just for you!' she snapped. 'That's my dinner.'

I let go. 'I know,' I mumbled.

She tore a piece. Her face was tight. I was thinking this was crap. I wanted to go back living with my da. She ate and said, 'I've never talked to you about babies.'

'What are they?' I said.

'Babies?' she smiled.

'What?' I said.

For the rest of that evening we sat in the room doing nothing. I could hear her breathing. It was getting on my nerves. I put Samantha's flowers in a milk bottle and put it on the windowsill. It was a boring evening. My ma got into the bed. I fiddled about because I didn't fancy getting in. Then I got in.

A few nights later we got beer in. While she was carrying the fire up I had to tape round the window to keep her happy. Then we began to lie around the room drinking beer. By now we had done the room up. Over the old wallpaper she had stuck up pictures from magazines of smiling babies. They cheered up the room. They added to the old limey wallpaper. We weren't talking much. We just sipped beer. I was sitting on the floor with Samantha's flowers spread on the carpet. I wanted to arrange them all more prettily in the milk bottle. My ma was on the floor goggling at me for some time before at last she said, 'You might as well know.'

With a flower in my hand I said, 'Can I play a tape?' I pulled out my radio-cassette from under the bed. I said, 'Do you like Simon and Garfunkle?'

She reached over and put her hand on the top of the radio-cassette and said, 'In a minute.'

I went back to the flowers. They were very bright and different. It was like they were smiling. It was like they didn't know why they were in a strange room. I lay the same ones together.

She said, 'Do you want to hear something mad?' I twiggled the petals. I knew I was going to be embarrassed. I smiled and said, 'Not really.' She leaned over and tickled me with a big red hand. I squealed and fell back. We both giggled until she tried to look serious. 'Listen,' she said straightening her face. I sat up. I took a rose bud in my fingers. 'Things are going to be different from now on,' she said in a serious voice. The bud was soft. She may have been waiting for me to ask why. I fiddled inside the bud. After a pause she said, 'We're going to have another person.' She suddenly laughed loud and looked puzzled.

I looked down at the petals and said, 'In this room?'

'Paul,' she said. I didn't answer. It was mad to put my finger right inside the bud. She sipped from her can. 'I have to tell you.' She smiled in a stupid way. Then she said, 'I'm going to have a baby.' I was getting a hard-on by fiddling inside the bud.

She asked me had I heard what she had just said. We heard the blue siren of an ambulance. Now I needed to grin. 'Now, Paul,' she said. I lay back. I didn't want to giggle. I rolled on my side and held my other side. 'Don't go flipping out on me,' she said. When she said that I stopped. I rolled back round. I lay looking at her.

'Who taught you to say that word?' I frowned at her. 'Flip,' I said. She asked me did I understand what she had just tried to tell me. I said, 'When?' She said I had to be responsible.

'You could live as the daddy.'

I stayed on the floor. 'What do you mean?' I said. 'Like my da?'

She said, 'Yeah,' and sipped from her can. I thought about that. 'The cot could go there,' she said. There was a limey silence for a moment. The hard-on had gone away.

'What would that make you?' I asked. 'Like a granny?'

'Paul.'

I said, 'Would you be?'

She whispered, 'Listen.'

'Could my bird live with us?' She didn't answer. She was looking serious again. 'She could be like the ma.' She didn't answer again so I picked a flower up and slotted it in the vase. I asked her how she knew it was only one person anyway. She was concentrating. There were four flowers the same. It was lovely how they were pink and identical. I fiddled with them to see what would happen. 'What if you had four people?' I laughed.

'Paul,' she whispered.

'Sextuplets.'

Her head made a tiny shake. I lay flowers in my arms like a baby. I couldn't keep my face straight. I began to cradle the flowers. 'Oh Christ!' she began to laugh. She dropped her head with a laugh. 'Stop it.' I lay back. We both cracked up. She held her side. It was very joky. Then we sat looking at the room and panting. Our laughs died away. It was quiet. The sink gurgled. All of a sudden she said, 'I'm depressed.'

I sat up. I jabbed all the flowers into the milk bottle. I got up and put it on the windowsill. I sat down. She whispered, 'I think there's someone out on the stairs.' We went silent.

Rain blew against the window. I needed to go to the toilet.

She got to her feet. She flumped down on the edge of the bed. 'Paul,' she whispered.

'What?'

Her face squashed up. 'This is crap.' Tears started to drip off her eyes. I sat on the bed beside her.

'You're depressed,' I said. I made my voice soft. 'That's natural.'

'What do you know?' she sobbed. I sat. There was a burp from the flat below. She mumbled, 'What'll I do?'

'What do you want to do?'

'Not have it!' she cried loudly.

I shrugged my shoulders. 'Don't have it then.'

She nodded after a bit. She wiped her eyes and looked at me with her face. 'What would I do on my own? I mean, like you can just see me . . .'

'You're not on your own,' I said in a cheery way. The flowers were cheery. I reached for my can and took another slug. She said, 'God help us,' and then I said, 'What'll we do now?' She breathed out loudly.

'Get into the bed.'

I said I needed a piss. We both looked over at the door. I didn't fancy going out to the stairs on my own and seeing the person. She said she would come too. She took a small sip of her beer. She spilled some. Then we went out to the stairs together. There was no person. We went down to the bathroom. It was chilly cold. She waited outside the toilet for me. I couldn't stop pissing in a loud way. Then we hurried back up into the room. Quickly we got into the bed. 'Night night,' she said. 'Night night,' I said. The bed squeaked every time we moved. I felt her legs touching mine. A bell was donging far away. She took up a lot of room and the blankets kept slipping off.

A day or two later I walked through town hoping to find

Samantha selling flowers. It was cold and bright. I did see her. She had a pram with boards over it. She was standing behind it shouting out the names of the flowers on her board with lovely pink cheeks. I stopped in front of her. 'How much are your bouquets?' I asked. She grinned. Smoke came out of our mouths. I went behind the pram. We kissed deeply in front of everyone on the street. She whispered into my mouth, 'You owe me for one.'

A woman stopped. She wanted to buy flowers so I stood back a moment. The woman put her nose close to the flowers. I mumbled, 'I didn't buy it off you, you gave it away.' When the woman walked off with a bunch I stood behind Samantha and put my lips on her neck. She leaned her head back on my shoulder. 'Good news,' I said softly. She smiled up at my eyes and whispered, 'What?' 'My ma's going to have an abortion,' I said.

I saw her blink upside down. It looked mad. She stood up straight. She faced me and said, 'What?' An old man was examining flowers.

'My ma's pregnant. I forgot to tell you.' The man asked about the flowers. I said, 'She's having a person.'

She didn't laugh. She turned round to the man. A tear dripped down her cheek. The man shouted, 'How much are your chrysanths?' He had a tall head. She told him. He pinched the petals.

'What's wrong?' I said.

She said under her breath, 'Nice chrysanths.' She pretended to look all over the sky. The man handed her money. She counted his change and her hands trembled. She glanced at me.

'You bastard,' she breathed. The tear was on her lip.

'Why?' I said.

The man shouted, 'How much are they each?' She answered

weakly, 'Fifty.' He fingered and thumbed the chrysanths. She turned her head to me. 'Is it yours?' she said.

'What!' I said. The man walked away with his bunch.

'You sleep in the same bed.'

'So what?' I shouted back. 'Do you think I'm riding my ma or something?'

'You sleep with her.' She scowled. 'Don't you? You can't say you don't!' Her cheeks had got pinker and cheekier. 'She doesn't live with your da.'

'So?' I said. I wanted to kiss her again. 'She rode someone else then. Is it any of your business?'

'It is,' she said and added quietly, 'if she's having an abortion.'

I took her fingers. They were warm. I wanted to suck them. 'Do you not want to do it then?' My hand fiddled with her hand. It was moist and soft. 'When she's out?' Her hand was getting me horny. 'At her abortion?' She asked why my ma didn't live with the man. I got closer to her. I said, 'How should I know?' I took a flower from one of her bunches. 'Ask her.' I brushed her ear with the flower. That got me flustered.

'You don't love me,' she said.

'I do.' She did a shrug. I put the flower under her chin. I tried to say in a sexy way, 'Are we doing it?' She made an Mmm sound. I kissed her again and imitated her Mmm. 'I'll come over for you,' I said. 'Could be tomorrow.' I walked in front of the pram. 'Right?'

'Yeah,' she said. She smiled and touched her chin. I backed away into the crowd. The sky was an apricoty colour. I nearly could taste it. The clouds were blue.

Late that night in the room my ma cleared her throat and said, 'I have to see someone tomorrow.' She was on her knees in front of the fire. The dark in the room smelled like smoke. I said, 'Do you? What for?' She said, 'Well.' She got up on her feet. She shivered a bit with the cold. I sat down on the wobbly chair.

She stood and glared at me. 'I suppose you know what an abortion is?' she said. I tried to hide my smile. She looked straight at me with a cross face and said, 'Your ma's going to have an abortion!' like it was my fault. I raised my eyebrows and whispered, 'Shit!' Then she said, 'We'll have to go early.' I didn't say anything.

She crossed the room and put her hands on a new canister of gas. She heaved it up straightening her back. She swayed with it from foot to foot, then stopped. She panted, 'Very rough,' and rolled it over to near the bed. She straightened up again and panted, 'Not a safe area.' She connected the fire.

'I don't want to go,' I said.

Her face got planky. She went and bounced down on the bed. She was getting her breath back. 'We've only,' she shouted with her eyelids down, 'one key!'

'I don't agree with it,' I told her. She put her hand on her face. She covered her eyes. 'I don't want to stand around,' I said. There was a laugh in the flat underneath us. 'When it's happening.' I glimpsed her face crumpled up behind her hand.

'I try,' she began to sob. 'For what fucking reason?' I got up to look for something in our grocery box. I didn't agree with my ma saying fuck. 'I am thirty-nine!' she yelled at me.

'What am I getting blemt on it for?' I shouted back. 'It's nothing to do with me. I don't want to see your abortion!'

She pressed her shoes off in a furious way with her feet. She wiped her eyes and seethed, 'It's just to see about it first!' I rummaged in the grocery box. There was nothing to eat. 'I can go back on my own then even.' Just then I heard her unzip her dress. In the mirror of the wardrobe I could see part of her undressing. I stood like I was searching in the box to give her time to take off her dress and put on her nightie. Samantha came into my head pulling her blouse over her arms in her bedroom and rubbing cream on a pimple underneath her breast. 'I rub cream on it.' My stomach went upside down.

'Oh,' I said from the box. I made noises in it. 'If it's a tough area.' There was a crescent of a moon in the mirror. When she was in her nightie I went back to the chair. 'I'd have to go with you,' I said. The room was warming up. 'Till you know your way.' She stood up to get into the bed. I asked her before she got into the bed would she go out of the room and let me change my Y-fronts. She went and stood outside the door. Quickly I took a pair from a plastic bag with my clothes in it. I stood against the door to stop her coming in. When I had stumbled into the new pair I took my cock and jerked it fast. I tried to see the pimple on Samantha again. I couldn't get a good hard-on now. I kept rubbing. My ma shivered outside. 'Bleeding hurry up!' she called. I called, 'Right,' and skipped over and into the bed. She came in. She fell against the door to close it. She turned the fire off and the light off and got in. The building was quiet. She gave a big sigh. Now and again the tap spurted.

The next morning I woke up wanking. I could see Samantha wobbling her bare arse in front of my face. I stopped when I knew where I was. I listened to find out if my ma was awake and if she knew. Her face was right against mine and her elbow was in my back. I slipped out of bed and quickly pulled on my jeans. I could smell Samantha's flowers in the room. I changed the water in the milk bottle to keep them blooming. Their cheeriness was like Samantha's cheeks. It was like they still didn't know this was a crap room they were taken to. I sat on the wobbly chair gazing at the old wallpaper and seeing legs in the pattern lit up by the sun. My ma stirred. She asked what time it was. 'We have to get up and out,' she said in a weary way. I said, 'Where are you going?' She didn't react.

As we set off she was clutching her purse. A dog was licking a squashed tomato. Up a lane was a church in the mist. We walked down to the river to get a bus. As we were walking she took a bit of paper out of her purse. An address was on it and a drawing of tower blocks and an X on one of them. We got to the quay. We waited for a bus just outside the shop with the beds. This time we were the only ones waiting. She looked in the window of a baby shop at cots. The mirrors and plants were out again. A bus came. We got on. The driver thinned his eyes at us so we sat upstairs. As the bus took us through the streets we talked. My ma didn't look very jokeful but she started to crack jokes. I was thinking about Samantha expecting me to call round. Everything was smudgey in the mist. We got a bit excited. At last we made out the tower blocks from the window. We got down off the bus.

The ground was flat. Ahead of us lots of towers were sticking up. We passed the first two towers and a gang. A baby was on a tricycle. As the next towers came near a bunch of kids of different sizes watched us. Some skipped over a tiny wall and ran up to us. Their faces were similar and very facey. They wanted to know who we were looking for. I shouted back, 'No one, right?' but when we were a distance from them they sang the music of Laurel and Hardy. My ma checked the bit of paper again and muttered, 'God forgive us.' We went into the next tower. We found the lift. The tower stank of piss. My ma said, 'She mightn't be in.' The lift opened. There was a greasy chip paper in the lift. We ignored it. We went up almost to the top. The lift opened again and we stepped out into dank. We whispered. The walls were decorated with graffiti. We tiptoed in front of the doors inspecting the numbers. A baby cried from behind one of them. The doors were metal. 'This is it,' my ma said. I walked to her. We stood outside a door. Before knocking it she checked the bit of paper again and stuffed it in her purse and clicked it. We could hear kids inside.

'Go,' I said.

'You,' she said. We stood for a few moments feeling giggly. Then I pushed her and ran back up the corridor giggling. She panted up after me to the stairs. We held in squeals. We didn't want to knock. We were going to go back on the bus. 'Have some sense,' she told herself. We walked finally down again and knocked.

A dog started to yap. A woman called out, 'Who is it?' My ma called that she was calling to see her. She said a name. The door cracked open. The women was frail. She shouted to the dog to stop snarling. She let us into the flat. Then the dog flipped about in a crazy way. It was skinny and frowned at us. In the main room kids were on the floor gawking at us. They were eating wedges of bread in front of a telly. I could see the city through the window behind them in mist. We went into the kitchen and stood. The skinny dog's lip was sticking up. It really wanted us out. The woman said, 'Yis don't want it?' She had a packet of peanuts. Her eyes were red and her hair was like a boy's. We didn't reply. Then she said carefully, 'I'll need something now,' and took peanuts. My ma fidgeted and said, 'How much?' There was a bit of a peanut on the woman's wrist. Then a small girl came and stood in the doorway. She was naked.

When I saw her I wanted to not be there. She was all pink with long straight hair. The woman munched her peanuts in a worried way. I felt my ma shift. The woman said, 'Give us twenty.' The skinny dog grunted. The girl put a finger between her legs. I stared at the table. It was covered with dirty cutlery and things. There was butter and a toy soldier and sweet wrappers. Some sun speckled the things. My ma started to take out money. Then the woman noticed the girl. 'Go and put some clothes on!' she bawled. The girl darted away. Her arse bobbed into another room. I turned and looked through the window while the woman said things. The city was a milky blur. I had a big hard-on.

The skinny dog growled again behind me. The woman asked my ma could she come back tomorrow afternoon. I looked down at the skinny dog. I didn't like the lip. It was an evil lip. The kids had started to make noise in the large room. The woman went out for a second wiping her hands on her jeans. I looked at my ma. I mumbled, 'Don't worry, it'll go all right.' The skinny dog's lip was still up. My ma clasped my arm. 'Come on,' she said. The skinny dog barked. We made a move forward. Then there was a scream. The skinny dog was biting on my ma.

My hand jumped to a knife on the table. The handle was gone. I got jam on my hand. My ma had backed a bit and the skinny dog was facing her snarling. I didn't know what to do. I decided to kick. It shot out of the kitchen just like that. The woman came back in past it. She cried, 'Did he bite you?' She spun round on her heels. 'That pox.' She went away again.

My ma looked at me. 'Come on,' she said with an important voice. I scraped my hand along the edge of the table to get off the jam. From the other room the woman shouted, 'I'm sick of that thing in the gaff.' We walked out of the kitchen. All the kids started to shout. We caught sight of the woman through the doorway of the main room trying to pick up the skinny dog. The kids danced in the speckled room. We opened the door of the flat and went out into the corridor. 'John!' we heard from inside. 'Open that fucking window!' The kids were screaming as we nipped into the stairs. I followed my ma all the way down the stairs of the tower and out into the air.

She gasped. 'Your leg?' I asked. She sat against the tower resting. She shook her head. I squinted up in case the dog would drop out the window. After a bit we got up and walked back past the other towers to the place for the bus. We waited for a bus. The day was pale. It was good we were going through with it.

Going back in the bus she had a pale face. We got off the

bus by the river. On our way to the room I tried to get her to speak. I stretched my arm around her shoulders. We were passing a church ground with railings. 'Get some beer,' I suggested. I gave her a small pat on her back but she looked at me and sighed, 'Wise up.' I mumbled, 'Celebrate.' The trees were scraping the white sky. They were shrivelled up and webby. We just walked. Just before coming to the door facing the fruit market on Mary's Lane I said, 'Well I'm getting some with my money.' I walked towards a pub on the corner.

'All right,' she grumbled, 'I'm coming.' We went into it.

Up in the room it was cold. She snapped the fire on. I set a can on the ground for her. I opened a can and got on to the bed. I put all my tapes on my lap and rattled through them to choose one to play. She washed dishes under the tap. Some men shouted on the lane below. She began to dry the dishes powerfully with a cloth. 'What's wrong?' I said. She didn't speak. 'Sit down.' I moved my legs to make room on the bed. 'Celebrate, why don't you!' I felt like being glad. The smiling babies and Samantha's flowers made me feel happy. 'Enjoy life.' She flapped the tea towel down by her side.

'From tomorrow,' she said slowly, 'I need you to help me more.'

'Okay,' I mumbled. A wet crumb was clinging on her cheek. She took out a pan. I swallowed beer.

'We'll have a hard time managing.'

I nodded my head agreeing. 'Why?' I said.

She tried to hide a small smile. She came over to the bed. She sat down. She shook my knee with her big hand. 'I'm going to keep it,' she said.

I lolled my head back against the wall. She got up again. She went over to the oven. She turned it on. 'Good,' I said softly. I started to think of Samantha. I imagined us going round the back of a church. I saw her with her top off saying, 'I'm not taking my bra off,' while I poked her belly button. I got worried about how hard it would be to coax her. My fingers trembled thinking of her. My ma took out a knife. I couldn't think how I could get Samantha to do it. I bit the rim of my can. I wanted to say something to break the silence. My ma began to tap the knife against an egg. 'You know,' I said. I set my can on the floor beside me. 'Sitting here like this in this dump . . .' I took my can up again. She didn't stop tapping. 'I could really hate you.' I spoke in a sensible way. 'You know what I mean?' She tapped more lightly and went, 'Mm, that's normal.' After a moment I said, 'That doesn't annoy you, does it?' She put down the egg. I looked into my can. 'That I hate you?' I heard her put down the knife. When I looked over at her I noticed that she was smiling with very wide eyes. My heart got fast. That face was a surprise to me. She made another face to herself. I didn't like that. I sprang to my feet.

As I put on my shoes and jacket she didn't look at me. I muttered, 'I forgot something.' I lifted another can. Then suddenly she laughed a scream. I flinched. I hurried to the door. I went out muttering, 'See you.' I went down the staircase with the can. Then above me I heard her scream, 'Walk out, then!' I looked up. She ran out to the stair rail trying to spit down quickly.

I kicked the leaves on the way to my bird's flat. It was gusty. The streets were orangey and dark. I picked up a chestnut getting the idea of throwing it at her window. It was like her tit. I threw it. I hit the window. It was a flukesome hit. I walked into the flats and up the stairs. She was standing at her open door when I got up. I coaxed her out into the corridor. I spoke with my mouth right up to her cheek. 'Let's do it behind a church,' I whispered. I smelled her.

'You're pissed,' she said.

'Come on.'

She said, 'No.'

'What's wrong?' I asked her. My hands held her waist. 'Can we not do it behind a church?' I pulled up her sweater.

'I don't believe in that abortion,' she said.

I said, 'Don't have one then.'

'You'd just leave me.' I let go of her. I walked up against one of the walls and took a slug of beer.

'How do I know,' she asked, 'you wouldn't just walk off?' I rapped my heel against the wall. There was a big cock scrawled on it.

'You don't know,' I said, pretending to not care. 'You'll just have to trust me.' She joined me by the wall. I dented my can in and out with one hand. Then she put her arms over my shoulders.

'Would you have my baby?' she asked in a soft way. I got butterflies.

'Come on,' I said. I took her hand and pulled her towards the lift. Her hand was warm. She asked me what I was doing. 'Come on and have your baby,' I said.

'It's just sex you're after!'

I said what was wrong with sex? I had her with one hand and said to come into the lift.

'I'm not doing it in a lift.'

'Would you not?' I said. 'It'll only take a second.'

'Fuck,' she said, 'it's not romantic.'

'Samantha.' My fingers were rubbing up and down her fingers and her wart. She said we could do it when we got a bed. A slam echoed far away. 'Well just come into the lift and talk about it then,' I said, but she walked over to her door. From the lift I asked, 'Can I not talk to you for a minute?'

She said, 'You're talking to me.' She played with her fingers.

'In private.' She leaned in her doorway. I said her name.

'No,' she said. There was a muffled shout from the staircase.

I walked over to her. 'Would you not, Samantha?' I took her hand. 'Come on.' She said, 'No.' Then I heaved her towards me by her hand.

She screamed and fell to her hunkers.

'Would you not?' I dropped my can. She cried. 'I just want to talk to you,' I said quietly. She struggled with my hand. 'Just talk to you.'

She cried, 'No.' She broke her hand free and lay back on the ground weeping.

'Would you not?' I poked the button on the lift. I grabbed her wrist. She screamed again. My arm trailed her an inch. 'Would you not?' She managed to get up on her feet, crying. I still held her wrist. 'Have your fucking baby!' I said. She got free. 'Have your baby, come on.' But she hurried into her flat. 'Samantha!' She slammed the door. She bolted it. The lift opened with a clang. 'I'm sorry!' I shouted in to her. 'I'm fucking sorry, right?' I went into the lift and down to the ground. I walked out of the flats and back to the room.

The door on the lane was open for me. My ma was in bed when I got back. She made room for me in it. I took off my jeans and went over to it. I squeezed into it. I tried to lie near the edge. I tried to not creak. For some time I couldn't get out of my mind the thought that Samantha might have come into the lift with me. As I was imagining my ma spoke into the dark. 'We'll get a bigger flat, Paul.' I didn't move. 'It's too small for three.'

I thought for a bit. Then I mumbled, 'It doesn't matter to me. I'll be getting my own flat soon.'

She rolled to look at my back. After a minute she said, 'I need you to help me.' I didn't give an answer. 'Like a daddy.' I heard her voice break. I wanted her to stop talking and let me imagine. 'I need you near,' she started to cry.

'That's nice,' I said. 'Because I'm fucking sick of the sight of you.' She rolled over again. Very soon I went to sleep.

*

The next morning when I stirred my ma was already up and dressed. 'Get up, Paul,' she said. She was moving around the room. 'We've got some talking to do before I go out.' Her voice was deep. I rubbed into my eyes. I remembered what I had done to Samantha and felt crap.

'Tell me here,' I muttered on to the pillow. I glimpsed her. She put on her coat. She sat down on the wobbly chair. I rolled on to my back and looked at her. There was a colourful smell from the bouquet.

'I need you to pull your weight,' she said quietly. Her face was worried. 'Do things. Do you understand?' I got a tingling all over. 'Mm.'

She picked up her purse. 'Help me,' she said. She bent down. 'Do the fire.' She reached out for her shoes. 'Get up, will you?' I stretched out in the bed. 'I want you to get some messages.' I started to get flustered thinking of Samantha coming up the stairs with me. 'I won't be well when I get back,' she said. I wasn't listening. Samantha would sit down and start to take her clothes off. 'Do you understand?' My ma was louder. I grunted. A church was ringing far away. I knew that Samantha could be sitting with lovely pink legs on the wobbly chair that afternoon. She would stand and take her bra off and take her pants off and whisper in my ear, 'Will you have my baby?' My cock was warm and slippery against the sheet. She would slip into bed beside me. Her arse would be lovely and soft. I would give her her baby and we would all be happy. 'Get up!' my ma shouted. She looked out at the wind.

'You don't have to shout,' I told her. A leaf blew against the window. 'I'm getting up.'

◇